D0874340

Afrolantica Legacies

Afrolantica Legacies

Derrick Bell

Third World Press
Chicago

Copyright © 1998 by Derrick Bell

Printed in the United States of America

First Edition 1998

04 03 02 01 00 99 98 5 4 3 2 1

Cover Art and Design by Niki M. Mitchell

Library of Congress Cataloging-in-Publication Data

Bell, Derrick A.
    Afrolantica legacies / by Derrick Bell.
        p.   cm.
    Includes bibliographical references.
    ISBN: 0-88378-199-9 (cloth : alk. paper).
    ISBN: 0-88378-200-6 (pbk. : alk. paper).
    1. Afro-Americans—Civil rights. 2. Afro-Americans—Politics and government. 3. Racism—United States. 4. United States—Race relations.
    I. title.

E185.615.B88 1998
305.896'073—dc21
                                                97-35807
                                                    CIP

Third World Press
P.O. Box 19730
Chicago, IL 60619

Epigraph

"Geneva, suppose Thomas Jefferson stepped out of history and suddenly appeared before me, and it was my task to bring him up to date on the technological developments of the last two centuries. Where should I start: with airplanes, computers, television?"

"First," she responded gently, "you would have to explain to Jefferson how you, a black man, had gotten free of your chains and gained the audacity to try and teach a white man anything."

Table of Contents

Prologue

Afrolantica rose slowly, majestically, fully formed from watery depths in about the location of the mythical, lost continent of Atlantis. From afar, the beauty of its vista offered immeasurable bounties. Explorers from around the world, eager to claim this new land for their countries, learned, after near tragedies, that, try as they might, they could not survive in its heavy and oppressive atmosphere. Afrolantica appeared an appropriate name for the miraculous new land following the discovery that only African Americans were able to breathe and survive there. The first black visitors reported a sense of well-being, a "euphoria of freedom" one called it, that they had never known in America.

For millions of African Americans, the news was a revelation, a new birth. Here was the long-sought promised land available to them in this life. There they could build a new society, one free of the racial hostility that in its many forms had so debilitated their efforts to survive in America. Millions of blacks were determined to move to this new land, to begin an ideal society. Joining together in an unprecedented cooperative effort, they organized and implemented the Afrolantica Armada.

Their rallying cry was: "Anyplace but here," the same slogan that had spurred so many of their nineteenth century forebears who determined to immigrate to Canada, Mexico, or back to Africa. Strangely, it angered those whites who had been most vocal in opposition to civil rights initiatives. Now, with blacks actually planning to leave, they sponsored government resistance maneuvers intend- ed to discourage blacks from emigrating—harassing leaders of the movement, and threatening a loss of citizenship to those who set sail on the Afrolantica Armada. Official opposition served as reassurance to the emigrants. They were doing the right thing.

The pleadings of relatives and friends who were not going was more difficult to turn aside, but early on a sunny Fourth of July morning, a thousand ships filled with the first wave of several hundred thousand black settlers set sail. As they approached Afrolantica, its beckoning lands were surrounded by thick mists, and the sea was disturbed by rumblings from the deep. Suddenly, the mists dissipated to reveal Afrolantica sinking back to the ocean's bottom.

They watched the last tip of the great land mass slip beneath the waves. Shocked, saddened, they gathered, grieving and praying for strength, for understanding. Why, when they had invested so much should it all come to nothing? Where was the meaning in this destruction of their hopes? What had they done to warrant this devastation of their dreams?

Then, as the ships swung around to take them back to America, the miracle that was Afrolantica was replaced by a greater miracle. Slowly at first, and then with increasing certainty, the black men and women on board the armada realized that their dis- appointment did not mean defeat. Though sobered by their loss, they felt deep satisfaction in having got- ten this far in their enterprise, in having accom- plished it together—despite the government barriers, despite the scoffing of friends. They discovered, as well, that they actually possessed the qualities of liberation they had hoped to realize on their new homeland. Experiencing this was, they all agreed, an Afrolantica Awakening, a liberation—not of place, but of mind. By the time the ships docked, the settlers were resolved. They understood the task that lay ahead, its difficulty, its far-from-certain outcome. The vision of Afrolantica they held so dear required continuing struggle here in an atmosphere unaccepting of their worth, uncaring of their needs, hostile to their very being. And yet they knew, actually they had always known, that those so willing to embrace every proof of black inferiority, so ready to adopt any rationale that kept blacks down, were themselves utterly dependent on the presence of blacks.

For without black people in America, what would it mean to be white? Of what value whiteness, the privilege of preference, the presumption of normality, the reassurance of majority status? Were the advantages of color to disappear, how would whites replace their carefully constructed but ever-fragile self-esteem based on whiteness? Blacks doubted that many whites would ever ask themselves these questions, but the questions were not less real because unacknowledged.

The returning black settlers recognized as well that the relationship of privilege based on color is two sided. Unless honored by those who are subordinated, it has no value for those who are dominant. This truth holds despite serious disparities in numbers, power, and wealth. The settlers saw this clearly, but how convey it to those they left behind who had not undergone the Afrolantica experience? They, too, would need counsel to nourish the continuing effort to transform subordination of the body into triumph of the spirit. In lengthy meetings, committees worked to fashion fundamental standards that would offer both inspiration as well as specific advice for everyday living. Finally, they presented and the settlers adopted what they hoped would serve as rules of racial preservation. They called them:

Afrolantica Legacies

I.

No matter how justified by the racial injustices they are intended to remedy, civil rights policies, including affirmative action, are implemented for blacks only when they further interests of whites. Thus, when society's rejection of a policy threatens progress toward our equality goals, that policy should be amended or replaced.

II.

Service in the cause of truth and justice is no less worthy of praise because it is misunderstood, misused, or condemned.

III.

Coalition building is an enterprise with valuable potential as long as its pursuit does not obscure the basic fact: nobody can free us but ourselves.

IV.

An individual whose actions against racism threaten the powerful must be prepared to endure both the condemnation of enemies and the abandonment by friends.

V.

Continued resistance by the powerless eventually triumphs over power, and thus oppression must be resisted, even when opposition seems useless.

VI.

The courage to confront racism, while worthy of praise, should not obscure the fact that the powerful can employ our confrontative statements to serve their ends as effectively as they can those deplorable self-blaming comments by blacks.

VII.

Life seems to favor those in power, while it seldom rewards triumphs with good works. The righteous must rely on their faith and champion justice even in a seemingly lost cause.

The determined humanity of our enslaved forebears is the foundation of the *Afrolantica Legacies*. It is not a gift that came with their color. It is the hard-earned result of efforts to make their way in a culture everlastingly hostile to their color. It is the quest for freedom and equality that has made survival possible and salvation achievable. An aspect of that survival, one that stretches toward the divine, is a perspective, an insight, and for some a prophetic power about this land and its people that is unique, a component of black art, an element of black character, a mainstay of black lives.

PART ONE
Racial Liberation Day

Racial Liberation Day
The Challenge for White Americans

L adies and Gentlemen. The President of the United States.

Good Evening:

Let me first thank the networks and the other media for providing this time on very short notice. As you will see, my request is justified by the information I want to share with you.

After several days of intensive investigation, government scientists working with the most advanced technologies have confirmed that a large land mass is moving up toward the surface of the Atlantic Ocean at a point roughly midway between the continents of North America and Africa. At its present rate of movement, it is expected to be visible within a few weeks and attain the size of Australia within a year.

From every indication, this appears to be the island called Afrolantica that emerged in about the same area several years ago. Its inviting topography turned out to be hostile to all but African Americans, whose emigration plans were frustrated when the island sank beneath the waves just as their ships were approaching. Scientists now estimate that if the island remains stable for six months, it will be a permanent part of the global geography.

Unfortunately, the conditions of racial exclusion and subordination based on color that prompted the initial emigration movement have not improved significantly and, in many areas, have grown worse. Many Americans point to the large, black middle class, the outstanding achievements members of the

3

group have made in many fields, their presence in neighborhoods, work areas, even television commercials, as proof that there are no barriers for blacks who are talented and qualified, and that racism is no more. These assessments wrongly dismiss the major gaps between blacks and whites in matters of employment, income, education and health care. They ignore the polls that show far larger numbers of blacks than whites who report that racism remains a pervasive presence in their lives.

Given these conditions, we must expect that if Afrolantica proves as inviting on its reappearance as it did initially, then in all likelihood, large numbers of African Americans will launch another emigration movement. Once begun, such a movement will be difficult to stop. Its ramifications will be damaging in the extreme.

I recognize that there are some Americans who believe the country would be better off without our black citizens. They are wrong. African Americans have made tremendous contributions to this society, many of them unrecognized, unappreciated, and unrewarded. The loss of these contributors would be great, but the reason for this loss, their departure because of the denial of opportunity and acceptance in this their homeland, would be greater, adversely affecting our leadership status abroad, and evoking a surge of shame and guilt with predictable recriminations. Internal disunity and strife at home could shake the moral foundations of a society that has prided itself, often excessively, on its melting pot of many races and ethnic groups.

I was not aware of the crisis posed by Afrolantica's possible return when, on June, 14, 1997, at the University of California, San Diego commencement ceremony, I urged the nation to begin a dialogue on race so that we might enter the twenty-first century as a unified, multiracial nation. I appointed a multiracial advisory panel headed by the eminent historian, Dr. John Hope Franklin, to help me launch a year-long discussion to determine what it means to be an American; not just in terms of the hyphens showing our ethnic origins, but in terms of our primary allegiance to the values America stands for and the values we live by. I warned that: "If during that year we do nothing more than talk, it will be interesting, but it won't be enough. If we do nothing more than propose disconnected acts of policy, it will be helpful, but it won't be enough."

As expected, the reaction to my race relations initiative was mixed. Some commended my statement, but felt I had not been sufficiently specific as to what Americans should do. Others felt that by saying anything at all, I was ignoring the progress the country has made, while stirring up racial differences that might better heal themselves over time. There was a range of views stretching between those urging me to either "do more," or "do nothing." Even those deeply concerned about the growing racial divide wondered whether my record—as opposed to my interest—in this field qualified me to lead a quest for a racial unity that has eluded the country for more than three hundred years. But I stand on my record.

In my first inaugural address, I called our racial divide, "America's curse." To set an example for the nation, I appointed a cabinet that would look like America. I named more minorities to high-level positions in government and to the federal judiciary than all my predecessors combined. I joined the tribute to Jackie Robinson, granted medals for the long-ignored black heroes of World War II, offered the nation's apology for the Tuskegee syphilis experiments, and strongly condemned racially motivated violence.

I also acknowledge my shortcomings in performance. I failed to defend Lani Guinier, a superb lawyer and a longtime friend, when in the wake of my nominating her as the Assistant Attorney General in the Justice Department's Civil Rights Division, she was subjected to a withering attack by conservatives whose charges were untrue, unfair, and a personal challenge to my integrity. I failed that test.

I should not have dismissed my Surgeon General, Dr. Jocelyn Elders, a courageous and competent public health physician and also a longtime friend. When she was subjected to vicious attacks for questioning the effectiveness of or our war on drugs policy, and then responding to a question at a health conference with the briefest and most common-sensical allusion to masturbation, I should have supported her. And during my first campaign for the presidency, it was simply wrong to embarrass the Rev. Jesse Jackson by criticizing statements of the rap singer, Sister Souljah, one of his conference guests at which I was also a guest. I want to publicly apologize for each of these actions.

In addition, as I indicated in my San Diego speech, I support affirmative action and regret California's enactment of Proposition 209 banning affirmative action in all state agencies and programs. But Proposition 209 might not have passed had I spoken out in opposition during my reelection campaign, when my leadership and the Democratic Party's money and muscle might have made a difference. Similarly, I did not come to the aid of the Black Congressional Caucus when—alarmed by the long prison terms being meted out to so many young, black men—they pleaded in vain with their congressional colleagues not to approve the federal law continuing far heavier penalties for those convicted of dealing in crack cocaine than its powdered equivalent.

I could continue. My point is that, like many of you, I do not have an unblemished record of active leadership in the race relations arena. My words have outstripped my deeds and often, as my critics make clear, my deeds have belied my words. In short, my policies on racial issues have mirrored this nation's. I have offered the symbolic gesture when it was popular or politically without cost, but I have not supported black people or their concerns when an election was at stake or other policies might be jeopardized by taking risks on their behalf.

I was made to see and regret the duality of my racial actions in an unscheduled but very valuable discussion with Ms. Geneva Crenshaw, a black, civil rights lawyer, widely known and greatly respected in the black community. Ms. Crenshaw convinced me that while my record has relied more on rhetoric than righteous action, acceptance of justified criticism is the necessary starting point of reform. She pointed out, moreover, that there are few well-known and living whites whose records of work in eliminating racism would justify giving them this responsibility. As your president, I view this as my duty and hope my example of active racial reform will serve as an example for many others who will join me to ease this long standing deficit of our democracy.

America has benefitted because our citizens or their parents came from every country and culture on Earth. But like so many countries, we tend to link along lines of easily recognized cultural attributes and to designate a group that is different as "the other," burdening members of that group with adverse treatment. I recognize, of course, that many

7

groups have experienced bias because of their race, ethnicity or religion, but only black Americans have been enslaved for two hundred years, segregated by law for almost another century and, in our time, given more the promise than the performance of equal opportunity.

It is beyond denial that our black citizens have borne the heavy burden of "the other" in our society. But it is not the burden of race discrimination on black people that I want to discuss this evening. It is, rather, the cost of that burden to whites. I don't mean the moral or ethical cost, though those are high. Rather, I want to talk about the economic and social disadvantage and lost opportunities that white people have suffered and continue to suffer as a result of the corrosive and pervasive effects of social neglect connected to race.

Economist Robert L. Heilbroner pointed out years ago that while the persons who suffer most from social neglect in America are disproportionately black, the merging of the racial issue with that of neglect serves as a rationalization for the policies of inaction that have characterized so much of the American response to need. Programs to improve slums are seen by many as programs to "subsidize" blacks; proposals to improve prisons are seen as measures to coddle black criminals; and so on. All too often, the fear and resentment of blacks take precedence over the social problem itself. The result, unfortunately, is that the entire society suffers from the results of a failure to correct social evils, whose ill effects refuse to obey the rules of segregation.[1]

Powerful entities in our society are able to convince a great many white people to think and act contrary to their best interests. They link the fact that a majority of America's population is white and most power is held by whites with a sense that, as whites, they are privileged and entitled to preference over people of color. Over time, these views have solidified into a kind of property—a property in whiteness. The law recognizes and protects this property right based on color, like any other property.

Scholars tell us that in a country that views property ownership as a measure of worth, many whites—with relatively little property of a traditional kind, money, securities, land—view their whiteness as a property right.[2] Professor Cheryl Harris asserts: "the valorization of whiteness as treasured property takes place in a society structured on racial caste. In ways so embedded that it is rarely apparent, the set of assumptions, privileges, and benefits that accompany the status of being white have become a valuable asset that whites sought to protect . . . whites have come to expect and rely on these benefits, and over time these expectations have been affirmed, legitimated, and protected in law."[3]

Professor Harris explains: "The wages of whiteness are available to all whites regardless of class position, even to those whites who are without power, money, or influence. Whiteness, the characteristic that distinguishes them from blacks, serves as compensation even to those who lack material wealth. It is the relative political advantage extended to whites, rather than actual economic gains, that are crucial to white workers."[4]

That political advantage over blacks, though, requires that whites not identify with blacks even on matters that transcend skin color. To give continued meaning to their whiteness, whites must identify with whites at the top of the economic pile, not with blacks with whom—save color—they have so much in common.

I want to give you just one example of what I am describing. Not long ago, I met a young man attending a law school where many students were from white working-class families. Most were the first in their families to attend law school and, like this young man, most were also opposed to affirmative action. This student felt he had made it on his own, and he told me that in his view "everyone—including black people—must make it on merit. That is the American way."

In response, I suggested that while he seemed quite able, he would have a hard time getting hired at large corporate law firms which prefer to hire students from Ivy League schools. Many of those students come from upper-class families. They weren't any smarter than he was; they were just born into richer families. Was that fair? My question stopped him cold. His eyes glazed over. Obviously, he had never considered the class disadvantage he suffered. After several moments, he said with a shrug: "Well, those are the breaks."

In other words, he was deeply suspicious of any black who got a job that he wanted. But if a white who benefitted from being born into an upper-class family got the job—he was ready to accept it. That was O.K. This attitude is widespread. It explains why there is so much opposition to affirmative action in college admissions, but none for legacy admits, the children of alumni or large contributors. Affirmative action based on family connections wins general approval even though more seats are taken by such students than those in which race was considered—and the alumni children overall do not have better academic credentials than the minority students.

And yet, it does not require prophetic power to

predict that if the law student is turned down for the job he seeks, he will harbor suspicions and resentment that some employers may build on by suggesting—usually untruthfully—that they had to give the job to a black candidate. More than one public official has gained office by suggesting that the job anxieties of whites are the fault of programs intended to remedy long-standing discrimination against blacks.

Unhappily, I can testify that blame can easily be cast in racial terms. When I signed the new welfare law promising to "end welfare as we know it," I exploited this race and social neglect syndrome as a campaign tactic that was effective because many Americans see an image of poor, black mothers when we speak of "ending welfare as we know it." They assume these black women—and their children—are unworthy of government support, and urge elimination of welfare even though the majority of mothers receiving federal welfare benefits are white. Under the new welfare law, blacks will be disproportionately affected, but the largest group, by far, who will lose benefits will be white.

But who are the major beneficiaries of government subsidies? Certainly, not the poor or the working class. Probably, home owners able to claim federal income deductions for mortgage interest and property taxes, enjoy one of the largest subsidies. Then there are the major corporations whom my former Secretary of Labor, Robert Reich, accurately identified as recipients of the major share of government welfare through defense contracts, agricultural supports, and a myriad of tax loopholes. And yet, because we focus on the occasional food stamp abuser, we don't recognize the enormous business profits made possible by government subsidies.[5]

This confusion of race and self-interest are not of

11

recent origin. It goes back to early colonial times. Historian Edmond Morgan explains that plantation owners convinced working-class whites to support slavery even though they could never compete with those who could afford slaves. Slave holders appealed to working-class whites, urging that because they were both white, they had to stand together against the threat of slave revolts or escapes. It worked. In their poverty, whites took out their frustrations by hating the slaves rather than the masters who held both black slave and free white in economic bondage. While slavery ended, the economic disadvantage—camouflaged by racial division—continued to work.[6]

During the latter half of the nineteenth century, a shared feeling of superiority to blacks was one of the few things that united a nation of immigrants, themselves horribly exploited by the mine, land and factory owners for whom they tolled long hours under brutal conditions for subsistence wages. Of course, many of these immigrants were far more recent arrivals than the blacks they mocked. The blackface and racially derogatory minstrel shows of that period helped immigrants acculturate and assimilate by inculcating a nationalism whose common theme was the disparagement of blacks, rather than uniting across racial lines to resist the exploitation and deprivation that do not respect any color line.[7]

The historic, according to scholar David Roediger, mirrors the present. The ideology of whiteness continues to oppress whites as well as blacks. It is employed to make whites settle for despair in politics and anguish in the daily grind of life. Roediger views the white woman campaigning for David Duke and "white rights" as just as much a victim of whiteness as her targets: the "blacks on welfare" whom she believes "get a new car every year." Unseating the loaded metaphorical associations of whiteness would free both blacks and whites, for it would confront racism as well as lead to the recovery of the "sense of oppression" in the white working class.[8]

Today, few whites would openly espouse racial superiority as the cause of their animosity toward blacks. They are not racists, they claim, because they are not prejudiced against black people. Many work with, live near, and are friendly with black people. What many do not recognize, however, is that racism is a system of continuing and cumulative advantage that benefits all whites whether or not they seek it. In America, whites are not simply in the majority. Whites hold most positions of power, own much of the wealth, and set most of the nation's policies; they are for all of these reasons the norm.

As a result, many of us do not think of ourselves as white, but simply normal. But being white provides a wide range of presumptions and assumptions that people of color may earn, but simply cannot assume. As Americans, we want to believe that our country is a meritocracy where anyone who has talent and works hard can be successful. Charges of racial discrimination threaten that image and, in all but the most blatant cases, many whites find it difficult to take them seriously. Thus, when blacks assert that racism is alive and flourishing, whites find denial is the easier, the more comforting reaction.

For these reasons, many whites live in denial about the advantages of whiteness and the disadvantages of blackness. A Gallup Poll reported that 58% of whites surveyed thought that the quality of life for black Americans had become better over the past decades, while only 33% of black respondents thought that it had. This large disparity in viewpoint reflects the refusal of many whites to face the reality with which blacks live. Those who assert against all the evidence that blacks are getting the best jobs and are doing better than whites need to examine the statistics of employment, income, health and wealth. They show that whites are far ahead of blacks by every measure.

Inaccurate assertions that racism is history nurture denial and serve as a connection across economic and other lines. Whites use the commonality of their resentment of blacks as adhesive, and that resentment blinds them to their class disadvantages. Racial denial and resentment, when fueled by economic anxiety, are combustible formulas for racial conflict that could seriously disrupt our nation at precisely the time when competing successfully in a global economy requires our cooperative energies and resources.

The current transformation of our economy holds the promise of a better, healthier, more fulfilling life for all Americans. But, in the transition, even as new industries are created, there is understandable anxiety as technology erodes millions of jobs. Embedded in this anxiety there is danger that many people will vent their unease and fear. We have gone that route before.

A century ago, when the U.S. economy was disrupted by the change from an agricultural to an industrial base, American blacks were already hated by large segments of society, particularly, hard-pressed farmers in the South and factory workers— many of them recent immigrants—in the North. Black people became the target for the wrath and frustration of white Americans squeezed by that change in job patterns. The history of racial disorders during the latter part of the nineteenth century and the early decades of the twentieth century are denoted as "race riots." In fact, many were uncontrolled massacres of innocent black citizens. No one would win, no one would be safe should such racial conflicts break out again.

Many conservatives, particularly those with radio and television programs, are fanning the flames of a potentially horrendous racial conflagration. They single out black crime, welfare rates, out-of-wedlock babies, dysfunctional families and communities, and conclude that "those people" do not deserve any help or sympathy. Conservative critics ignore data in Jeremy Rifkin's book, *The End of Work*, indicating that blacks have been hardest hit for more than two decades as the industrial era ended.[9]

These media demagogues ignore the disasters described in *When Work Disappears*, William Julius Wilson's book,[10] detailing how it is massive unemployment and not the lack of family values that has devastated so many black communities, placed one-third of young men—denied even menial jobs when they lacked education and skills—in prison or in the jaws of the criminal court system, most of them for nonviolent drug offenses.

Crime is a serious problem in the black and Hispanic ghettos, as it is among poorer whites, but no more so than it was in the England of Oliver Twist, or the France of Jean Valjean. The real culprit is unemployment. And yet, the media is not much interested in studies showing the high percentage of minority youth who are seduced into selling drugs because the labor market is closed to them. Seen through America's racial prism, black drug crime is viewed as a greater danger than the purveyors of tobacco, whose products kill 400,000 people a year and who are subsidized by the government rather than prosecuted. Similarly, affirmative action engenders more hostility from many whites than the fact that the top one percent of families now hold forty percent of the wealth—and the gap is growing. Such an environment fomented race riots in the past. Not even a mild paranoia is needed to imagine their return.

Practices of overt racism we thought consigned to history are reappearing with all their old virulence. In this period of economic transition, racial hostility could develop into the bloody conflicts that writer Carl Rowan describes in his sobering book, *The Coming Race War in America.*[11] Critics dismiss Mr. Rowan, but they have not come up with a more optimistic scenario, given the havoc created by joblessness among blacks. Millions of whites, their jobs gone or threatened, are venting their anger and anxiety on affirmative action and other programs they think unfairly aid black people.

My friends, there is no easy answer to the monster that race has been and remains in our society. Perhaps, nothing that I can do will ease or eliminate the danger it poses for all of us. But I will try, not through new civil rights legislation, or court suits, although I will take action to insure that the laws against unlawful discrimination are fully enforced. But the basic work must be done by every white person. We must each of us ask ourselves: "What can I do to ease the danger of racial conflict that threatens us all? What can I do to make Afrolantica a less attractive alternative for African Americans?" My friends, we can no longer afford whiteness as an assumed right of citizenship.

For those ready to join in this racial liberation crusade, there are several encouraging factors. My projection of the dangers we face from our continued adherence to more subtle but no less devastating practices of racial priority should not obscure the tremendous progress that we as a nation have made in the last three decades. Sociologist Howard Winant observes that U.S. society was once a nearly monolithic racial hierarchy, and while white power and privilege continue, racial identity and status are no longer identical. Indeed, even the determination of race by blood no longer makes sense—if it ever did. Most blacks have "white blood" and tens of millions of whites have "black blood." When you consider the intermixture of Latinos, Native Americans, and Asian Americans, both in this country and across the centuries, we are far more one people than our continuing racial conflicts would suggest.[12] The steady increase in interracial marriages and adoptions reflects the growing number of our citizens who are making the most sacred commitments across racial lines.[13]

Further progress is essential. The crusade to diminish race as a basis of privilege and priority is already underway. There are many antiracist, white groups who are meeting and placing into action plans to reduce the dangers and disadvantages of using whiteness as a measure of worth, a standard of normality. A national network of groups call themselves "Race Traitors." They reject loyalty to whiteness in favor of loyalty to humanity. Thus, if a white person tells a racist joke or story in a group of whites, a member of this group would say: "Oh, you must have told that story in front of me because you assume I am white. I am actually black and just look white. And let me tell you why I found that story offensive."[14]

Other whites are challenging the privileges of whiteness. At each instance of special treatment, they ask, "Would you have done this were I not white?" Whites, by refusing to accept without question the privileges of whiteness, begin the process of destabilizing that construction which society relies on to preserve the current system of racial subordination.

For those whites who are concerned but not ready to tackle the existing system so directly, there are courses and workshops where trained persons can help you understand and recognize the stages that social scientists suggest whites must undergo to rid themselves of a sense of guilt or denial in being white. These courses help replace long-held and often destructive myths with an acceptance of whiteness as an important part of oneself, and help develop a realistic and positive view of what it means to be white.[15]

If we are to get beyond race as a basis of status, the nation's whites at every level will have to wrestle with the question: If blackness does not mean subordinance, what does it really mean to be white, not as a matter of appropriate respect and pride in cultural heritage, but as a social and economic fact of life in these United States?

In our individual soul-searching, in our discussions with family and friends, we must begin an honest national debate about race. The subject of this debate is not blacks, their intelligence, their morality, their entitlement to rights, and all the other issues that usually monopolize our race discussions. Late in his too short life, Dr. Martin Luther King, Jr. observed that there have been plenty of studies of the effects of racism on African Americans. What is needed, King said, is a study of the effects of racism on whites.[16]

Well, we have the studies, but what we need to do is read and discuss them as scholars are doing in conferences, such as "The Making and Unmaking of Whiteness," held at the University of California.[17] That is why I am urging that the spotlight of the Great Race Debate must be focused where it belongs, where it should have been all along, on whites. The real issue, my friends, is not whether we are or are not racist. That term condemns rather than examines, closes dialogue rather than furthers debate. We must get beyond rhetoric, move beyond our assumptions, our long-held beliefs. Do we whites have enough love and respect and patriotism to remain a stable society without using blacks as a societal glue?

Dr. Martin Luther King, Jr. would have welcomed the call I am issuing this evening. Indeed, in preparing this speech, I spent many thoughtful hours with the writings of Dr. King. In the past, I have been taken to task—and correctly so—for suggesting what this great man might say were he to return and see the conditions in so many black communities. And so, I approached King's work with a new humility and gained from it a new insight.

During the balance of my presidency, Dr. King's life will serve as my model and my inspiration. In my quest to get this nation beyond its racial fixation, I expect to receive, as Dr. King did, criticism and condemnation. There may even be calls for my impeachment. The attacks may silence those who otherwise would join me in this quest, but I hope my actions energized by my public commitment will encourage many others to do as I am doing.

Our task is not easy, but neither is it impossible. The writer Alice Walker put it well. In a letter to me, she said: "The world, I believe, is easier to change than we think. And harder. Because the change begins with each of us saying to ourselves, and meaning it: I will not harm anyone or anything in this moment. Until, like recovering alcoholics, we can look back on an hour, a day, a week, a year, of comparative harmlessness."[18]

We may not succeed in our quest for racial liberation. I recognize the possibility of failure. But I think that our success is more likely if we are not afraid to fail in a righteous cause. The elimination of subordination of black Americans and white Americans based on differences of race is, I assure you, a righteous cause.

God bless you all and good night.

Racial Liberation Day
Geneva Crenshaw Responds

"Ladies and Gentlemen. In response to the President, Ms. Geneva Crenshaw."

Good evening:

We should all commend President Clinton for his candor in calling attention to this nation's dangerous addiction to color. As he points out, the reappearance of Afrolantica has given urgency to addressing this country's racial divide crisis. He correctly views the possibility of a large emigration of African Americans as a defeat, one from which the nation might not recover.

The President has appropriately aimed his speech at white Americans. In my response, I want to provide a perspective for black Americans and, indeed, all persons of color as the nation considers the President's call for white Americans to consider the benefits and the burdens of their whiteness. This is a historic event because it represents an official acknowledgment of the nation's racism and sets out a definition that encompasses all whites, not just the openly bigoted.

When Lincoln issued the Emancipation Proclamation, when the Supreme Court declared racial segregation unconstitutional, black people utilized these admissions of racial injustice to spark major drives toward freedom and equality. The President's Racial Liberation Address is of a similar character. While important as a call for soul-searching by whites, it can, as did those earlier acknowledgments, serve as a signal for bold actions by blacks.

It is appropriate for the President to urge white Americans to consider seriously the answer to his question: "How much are you willing to continue to pay, how much are you willing to continue to risk to preserve a property right in whiteness?"

This, though, is a question the answer to which is known to black people, indeed all people of color. It is foolhardy for black people to simply assume that the answer will differ from those we have been getting for over three centuries. Those answers were obvious when our forebears were exploited in slavery, degraded by segregation, and frustrated by the unmet promises of equal opportunity.

I depart from the President when he views this question as one mainly for whites. As in so many issues involving our rights and well-being, the President suggests that black people watch from the sidelines as whites discuss and enlighten themselves about race.

Mr. President, black people have been waiting for white people to get enlightened about race for a long time. We have watched as time and time again over this country's history, whites have chosen to protect their sense of belonging based on skin color over alliances with blacks that would have improved all of our lives. We have not been passive in seeking our rights but even our best efforts seem to translate into more property for whites and more promises for blacks.

Black people cannot afford to be passive on racial issues. For when we are, we miss a necessary, no, we miss an essential ingredient in the property in whiteness phenomenon. That ingredient is the recognition of white skin-color as property by we black people. Our recognition gives that property right its legitimacy. No property has value until others are willing to recognize that property, abide by its boundaries, refrain from trespassing its fences.

Ask the American Indians! They were here first and claimed occupancy of the land. It was by long usage, their property. Europeans were simply unwilling to recognize those property rights.

Ask our African ancestors! They lived in a different culture, one with its own values and customs and humanity. They certainly expected that they owned themselves. But Europeans built ships and through violent force, turned African humanity into human property and profit.

History provides proof beyond measure of the worthlessness of property when others refuse to grant it recognition or respect. Europeans have taught peoples of color that lesson all over the world. We need to apply it to our present condition. Believe me. Without our acquiescence, individually and as a group, the property right in whiteness would cease to exist. Think about it.

It is this property right that transforms all the myriad manifestations of racism from a monstrosity into a generally accepted norm. I tell you it is not normal that wildly disproportionate numbers of blacks die in infancy, live in poverty, are stuck in inadequate schools, hospitals, and prisons, work at minimum-wage jobs and reside in decaying communities. Only a commitment that white is right supports the myth that after three centuries of virulent racism, the nation's new-found belief in color blindness requires the immediate dismantling of affirmative action programs in college admission, in hiring, in voting.

Know that all these conditions and many similar

ones are components of white property. They are the cause of our deprivation, suffering, and death. Despite President Clinton's best efforts and those of many whites, the deprivation, suffering, and death of black people will continue as long as we give more credence to white property rights than we do to our own.

Yes, I know. You are saying that the Europeans had the guns and other weapons that enabled them to violate the property rights of Indians, Africans and other people of color. We blacks do not possess great firepower. No, but we possess a greater power. It is the power of ourselves. It is the power of right. It is the power that comes when we recognize that our salvation—not in Heaven, but right here on Earth—comes from a sense of pride in our self-worth. It comes when we determine not to sacrifice our self-worth in search of well-being or out of fear of loss. Recognition of self-worth provides a satisfaction that money can't buy and prestige can't protect.

Mahatma Gandhi knew that power and he used it to free India from the greatest colonial power of the time. Dr. Martin Luther King Jr. knew that power and was able to move us beyond the Jim Crow's subjugation that had been law and practice for the better part of a century. The power that ended state-supported segregation is still there. We can know that power.

We cannot effectively challenge property rights by whites by measuring our success, even our worth by our possessions and our happiness by our success. When measures of this character are totted up, they serve mainly to provide a surface legitimacy to the claims that racism is over and blacks can make it if they only stop complaining and get down to work.

Some may ask: "If whites must give up their

property right in whiteness, must blacks surrender our pride in blackness?" President Clinton answered that question when he distinguished property in whiteness from an appropriate pride in cultural heritage. And we have good reason for pride. Blackness is a concept distilled from the degradation of slavery and the exploitation of racism. It is a reminder that black and odious are not identical terms. The concept of blackness reassures us that we are worthy, despite the hostility to our presence we endure, the insensitivity to our pain we abide, and the inner rage we deflect—all too often on ourselves. Black pride, though, is more than a slogan. It stands as a symbol for our core values as a people, values that we must practice as well as preach.

These values include: self-respect earned through outreach to others, and recognition that black women are the key to our survival. We must support our institutions, schools, churches, and businesses, as viable vehicles for learning, worship, and economic development.

If we challenge property rights in whiteness, the very essence of racism, as our forebears challenged first slavery and then segregation, we, like they, can overcome the racial restraints of our time.

Thank you and good night.

Revelations

Across a seemingly endless expanse of white beach, the surf rolled in with a sound that softly lulled both eyes and ears. Beyond the scenic breakers, a calm sea flowed a pale green changing to a deeper and deeper blue until it merged with a sky across which cumulus clouds slowly promenaded, altogether the ideal setting for a vacation commercial.

I was seated on a spacious veranda located high above the beach. Directly beyond the railing, tropical flowers bloomed in brilliant displays. The veranda was attached to a large house, palatial in character. Behind the house as far as I could see, lay rolling green hills, interspersed with verdant plains. This could be the Caribbean, but the weather was in the low 70s, mild and invigorating.

Seated across from me on a long chaise lounge, her feet drawn up under her, a position that added depth to her more than six foot height, her black skin radiant as ever, her hair done in queenly braids wrapped round and round like a greying crown, was my friend of these many years, Geneva Crenshaw. Seeing that I was awake and surveying the scenery, she spoke quietly.

"Hello, friend."

Her conciliatory tone made me suspicious. "Geneva. Where are we?"

She smiled with that look of anticipation I had learned meant the answer would not be complementary.

"Let me put it like this. We are located in a far more pleasant place than most blacks get to who make a habit of trying to teach white folks anything."

27

"Meaning what?"

"Meaning, in general, just what I said. In particular, it means that after all the commotion engendered by the president's Liberation Day speech, I decided we both needed to be off the scene for awhile. And, as things are developing, I was right."

"But why? It seemed to me that his new speech replacing all those pleasant exhortations about race with the hard facts about white privilege and its high cost to its supposed beneficiaries is exactly what was needed to spark a long-overdue dialogue of substance on a subject that influences so much policy and is never acknowledged openly, much less discussed."

Geneva shook her head. "To date, there has been much more heated denial than thoughtful dialogue, I am afraid. More demonstrations demanding Clinton's impeachment and worse, than forthright debate. Beyond the noisy opposition though there is a quiet stirring—mostly missed by the media, of course. The demands for Clinton's head make better sound bites. But there is a quiet agitation, much of it coming from corporate leaders who know that if this debate gets violent, it will be bad for business."

"All you tell me indicates we should be there, right?"

"Wrong. Remember, our effort is to get whites to think about their investment in being white, and get blacks to see their role in making that investment profitable. Were we there, the public and certainly the media would gladly switch their attention to us and the nature of my influence on the president. I can hear the calls for FBI investigations, the congressional inquiries, the politically ambitious district attorneys indicting us for Lord knows what. You get the point."

"The point is that you have gotten me in hot

water again."

"Oh sure. Well, let's set the record straight for your fast-failing memory. You surely remember when I visited you shortly after Clinton gave his much-ballyhooed speech on race at the University of California, San Diego commencement. You were more than a little disappointed with all the hype and little more than a request that we get along. I wondered what exactly did you expect from a president many people consider the ultimate politician."

"And Geneva, as I told you at the time, he claims he wants to do big things during his second term, but getting his face on Mt. Rushmore will require more than political guile. It requires gumption and a willingness to support his programs in the face of overwhelming opposition. My frustration stemmed from the knowledge that despite all his policy disappointments, the president is able to act boldly, even courageously, as he did in sending troops to Haiti and Bosnia, and holding the line on the budget in the face of Republican threats to close down the federal government." I got up and started pacing in frustration.

"The challenge is to get the president to see that social change, when it comes, is borne on the scary wings of risk."

"Exactly," Geneva interjected. "And it was at that point that I suggested that you write the race relations speech the president should have delivered."

"And I did. Sure, I knew Clinton would face some political heat for a time—as Lincoln did when he issued the Emancipation Proclamation—but eventually the country will come to see that he did what was necessary to save the country. Just to test the reaction, I used what I wrote in a few lectures, advising my audiences that I had written the speech for the president. So, since you seem unable to share your schemes with me in advance, I was as shocked as every one else when Clinton actually issued that Liberation Day Order and mentioned you as the person who influenced him to speak out more specifically about race—and in my words. I don't think he changed anything. How did you manage it?"

Geneva gave me a devilish look. "Obviously, I had to use all my persuasive power even to get to see him and then convincing him took a bit more than persuasion."

"I knew it! Geneva. You used your powers to make Liberation Day happen. I thought your Curiae Sisters had forbidden you from actually influencing events here on Earth. It's what got you in trouble the last time you were here. Or . . . ," as I looked about my strange surroundings, "the last time you were in New York."

"True, but after I returned, I convinced one of them that what I did was necessary and the other sister, reluctantly, went along. So, I decided to put into effect what you said would be the start of a much-needed debate."

"And you simply assumed that I would not mind being whisked away from an exciting debate, and removed by God knows what means to wherever we are."

"Don't be so dramatic. Think about where you are."

I gazed out across the postcard-pretty vistas—the calm sea on one side, the rolling greet hills on the other. "This can't be Afrolantica?"

Geneva nodded. "You guessed it. It's Afrolantica, back from the ocean bottom for our exclusive use and beyond recognition by anyone else."

"But how can that be? The president reported

that scientists believe Afrolantica is rising, but that it remains below the ocean's surface."

Geneva was perturbed. "Are you going to listen to the white folks and reject the evidence you can see all around you? I won't bore you with the details, but just remember. Neither the president nor his scientists know everything. This is, indeed, Afrolantica. It will become apparent, real, and permanent when needed to shelter and provide for African Americans if the country of their birth proves unwilling to do so. In the meantime, relax and enjoy it."

"Easy for you to say, but hardly possible when the country is in an uproar over a speech I wrote. And what about my wife? Does she and my family know where I am?"

"They do and you can communicate with them whenever you like—and through means other than their tapped telephone lines."

"Very thoughtful; but damn, Geneva. Didn't you think you should have let me know what you were doing? This after-the-fact briefing is so typical. 'Do it now. Explain it later.' I am getting tired of it."

"I thought," Geneva replied calmly, "our relationship was based on trust, not on the expectation of full disclosure before either of us does what needs to be done. When you wrote the president's speech, I assumed that if you had the power to get him to actually give it, you would have used it. I have the power. I used it. Now, are you suggesting I misconstrued your wish that Clinton would deliver the to-the-point speech on race that you wrote?"

I looked at her and slowly shook my head. I sighed deeply. I wondered whether it was tougher to deal with Geneva's independence than her magical powers. "But wait a minute Madam, if you please. I wrote Clinton's speech, but how did you convince the networks to broadcast your response?"

She shrugged. "Well, you helped the white man say the right thing. I was simply serving as an equal opportunity speech provider for our people."

I shook my head. "So, how is Clinton bearing up under all the pressure and criticism?"

"So far, so good. It's not all been critical. Liberals and progressives hailed the speech. Predictably, conservatives viewed it as un-American and condemned Clinton for betraying his race. Leaders of the Christian Right have been calling on the president to recant or face damnation. To his credit, Clinton is sticking to his guns. He has been traveling all over the country repeating the themes of his speech and he has his cabinet doing the same. Democrats are of varying minds, but many have been surprised. A few beyond the Congressional Black Caucus even have said they are impressed by the president's strong leadership on the issue."

"How about working-class whites?"

"You know the answer to that. They are very resistive, though Lord knows, resistance and outrage are not limited to any socioeconomic level. If the president had to run again, he would face massive opposition, but he called for a debate on race, and he has certainly gotten his wish."

"And here I am languishing on Afrolantica that the world doesn't know exists."

"You will not be languishing, though, knowing your compulsive work habits as I do, a real vacation might do you a world of good. But I have a plan that should satisfy your need to work and make a long-distance contribution to the debate. In the original story about Afrolantica, as you know, after the settlers recovered from the trauma of watching their promised land sink back beneath the ocean's waves, they wrote a series of rules for racial preservation and called them *Afrolantica Legacies*."

I nodded, remembering. "Borne out of tragedy and despair, these rules pointed the way toward a rewarding life."

"True, and what I want you to do is help me generate a series of papers, some fiction, some essays, that will provide a written portrait of each of the seven *Afrolantica Legacies*. As we finish each writing, I'll transmit it back to the states where I have arranged for their publication and distribution. During the Great Race Debate, our papers will provide renewed purpose and give heightened insight to those who, despite all the 'trials and snares' have kept their eyes on the prize. Are you game?"

"I am always pleased for the chance to work with you, Geneva. But let's face it. I have published three books of our stories—well, your stories really—over the last decade and during that time, the condition of black people in the country has grown steadily worse. Even with your latest intervention and the resulting debate it has produced, it's hard to imagine how more of our writings can halt or even hinder the hostile forces arrayed against our people."

"The power of prophesy does not guarantee conversion. Most people reject predictions founded in truth as unreasonable, inconvenient, or frightening. That is why true prophets are more likely to be persecuted than praised."

"I understand that, Geneva, and it is why you have begun supplementing your prophesy with miraculous action. It certainly took a miracle to get Clinton, a politically cautious president if ever there was one, to take a stand on race far more radical than any of his predecessors. And, far from incidentally, you've made real for us a mythical land mass invisible to even the most advanced electronic surveillance."

"You make me blush," Geneva said with totally unconvincing modesty.

"I am serious, Geneva. Why don't you simply use those powers to convince blacks and whites of the debilitating effects of America's obsession with a property right in whiteness?"

"Believe it or not, friend, my powers are not without limits. I can influence individuals and we try to point the way through our stories, but people have to have choices. Otherwise, we simply substitute one form of domination with another. After all, even God does not deprive humans of free will—though given the shape of the world and the horrendous use so many make of their choices, God must be sorely tempted. I can intervene. And, at some level, anyone can. But even God can't—or won't—dictate ultimate outcomes. Understand?"

"I do," I acknowledged, still unconvinced about the value of more writing that even many black people don't read. "But our stories and their messages are rejected by some blacks as wallowing in black victimization intended to generate white guilt so that we can profit from whatever crumbs of appeasement whites offer."

"Give me a break, friend. Some whites claim we are ingrates for not agreeing with their claims that blacks are treated better here than in other countries with minority populations. You don't believe any of that and neither do I. It is tough for some blacks as well as whites to face up to the seriousness of their conditions. You are certainly not the first messenger who was denounced because you delivered bad news."

I sighed. "You're right, as usual. But Geneva, it

sure is tough trying to resist oppression with words and ideas. Trying to forestall the violence that seems the only thing that those in power understand."

"Friend, save the dramatics for our stories. Your office, computers, files and all, are set up just inside. Why don't you start with the first of the *Afrolantica Legacies*."

PART TWO

The Afrolantica Legacies

Chiara's Enlightenment

No matter how justified by the racial injustices they are intended to remedy, civil rights policies, including affirmative action, are implemented for blacks only when they further interests of whites. Thus, when society's rejection of a policy threatens progress toward our equality goals, that policy should be amended or replaced.

"Geneva, I think we should begin by alerting folks back home about what I fear is an unrealistic attitude about the future of affirmative action. There is, as proponents keep claiming, plenty of moral and legal justification for these programs,[1] and yet they are increasingly viewed as a dangerous form of discrimination by both the Supreme Court and much of the country. It is praiseworthy that civil rights advocates are digging in their heels, but—"

"Friend," Geneva interrupted, "I agree. Schools should insulate their diversity programs from political and judicial attack by eliminating racial and gender classifications by giving greater emphasis to characteristics we know from our affirmative action experience can predict academic success for many who do not have high grades and test scores."

"But don't forget. There are colleges that are quite ready to dismantle their special admissions programs rather than amend them."

"I know. Many of them have cut their minority admits without waiting for court orders. I am concerned now about those institutions who want to retain their affirmative action programs unchanged

39

despite adverse court orders. I remember a similar 'fight to the last man' attitude in the school desegregation struggle. What I urged civil rights advocates to do then was utilize the waning legal leverage of the 1954 *Brown v. Board of Education* decision to gain political support for new strategies that gave priority to educational effectiveness rather than simply assume that racially-balanced schools would achieve that result."

"For the most part, your advice was ignored until it was too late and many civil rights people felt you had sold out and abandoned the fight. And, now Mr. Glutton-for-Punishment, I take it you want to go the same route again."

"I don't enjoy criticism from civil rights advocates, Geneva, but affirmative action programs are now caught in a morass of opposition and uncertainty similar to that engendered by school desegregation programs. We need to recognize that and try to get sponsors to restructure the policies to insulate them from legal and political attack."

"You sound confident."

"I have support and enlightenment from a most interesting source. Let me tell you about it."

∽∾∽∾∽

July was approaching too quickly. My planned summer work load was not getting smaller, while the difficulties of preparing still another talk on affirmative action were getting larger. It would, I knew, be a challenge to say anything reassuring as one court after another found "constitutional flaws" in the programs. I found it frustrating trying to respond to opponents' claims that minority students admitted to colleges lowered academic standards. The critics seem uninterested in the studies showing that minority admits have about the same credentials as do so-called "legacy admits." That is, those students—mostly white—who get in because their parents are alumni or large contributors to the school.

To sort out my thoughts, I decided to get away from the office, the phone calls, the unscheduled visitors, and the endless requests that so preoccupy minority representatives at every professional level, enabling our colleagues to wonder—not always in complementary terms—why some minority teachers are so busy and yet seem to get so little accomplished.

I packed a lunch along with a briefcase and my trusty laptop computer, and drove out of the city and far off into the hills. Finding a quiet spot where nature's beauty has not been despoiled by strip malls and fast food franchises is increasingly difficult. I left my car on a narrow road that ended at the foot of an impressive hill and climbed to the top along a winding path. The day was clear and my view commanded a panorama of green fields and far-off towns.

I settled myself on a fallen log and dutifully spread out my work on a large, flat rock placed by nature conveniently at hand. I began typing my thoughts into the computer, and congratulated myself for choosing so felicitous a setting for work on the continuing enigma: affirmative action.

Happily engrossed in my work, I was more curious than alarmed when, glancing up, I noticed a parachute descending. I assumed it was a sky diver practicing this rather dangerous sport. Actually, at my age, I feel some envy for those so confident with life that they willingly defy death in their quest for excitement.

Strange, I thought, there was no plane visible in

the clear, blue sky, and no other sky divers. Meanwhile, the lone chute was getting closer. I could see the likely landing spot from my vantage place and observed that the chute touched down rather less gracefully than some I had seen. Small wonder though given the strange suit the jumper was wearing. It seemed metallic, gleamed brightly in the sun, and rather reminded me of the costumed space suits that might be worn in a high budget, Hollywood action film.

This scenic area seemed an unlikely place, I mused, for an advertising promotion. Then I smiled as I realized that we are so inured to the myriad manifestations of modern marketing that even the Second Coming would be greeted by most of us skeptically as simply a more ingenious means of gaining our jaded attention as a necessary prerequisite to separating us from our money.

There was little time to wonder about the interruption of my solitude. While I thought I was hidden from view, the newcomer quickly got free of the parachute, and headed directly for me, exuding as it approached so much peaceful cheerfulness that it would have been inhospitable to act on my first urge, which was to run as fast as I could in the opposite direction.

"Hail, Earth person," the being called. "I am Chiara." This being, while possessing a human's shape was quite clearly not of this world. The diction was impeccable, and the name calmed the ear like the flowing of a mountain stream.

"I have come from Nevus, a life star beyond your galaxy. There, our scholars are confounded by our study of your legal system and the long efforts of those who were brought here as slaves to gain the 'liberty, justice, and freedom for all' that according to your basic, legal documents are supposed to be the birthright of all who call themselves Americans."

"Damn." I thought to myself. "If studies of racial problems were the harbingers of change and not the substitutes for action they generally are, then there would be no need for this interplanetary visitor's long journey—or, for that matter, my need to be here trying to write positively about affirmative action, policies the society has created to give blacks the sense of equality while withholding its substance." Then, it occurred to me, "I had yet to say a word."

"Welcome," I said, holding up my open hand in a gesture intended to convey both greeting and peace. "Would you pronounce your name again."

"It is Chiara and would translate in your language to the word, chiaroscuro, meaning the arrangement of light and dark elements in a pictorial representation."

"I see," I nodded in understanding. "Are you a man or a woman? I can't see through the sun visor on your space helmet."

"Your question confirms the fixation on irrelevant gender differences. I am what you would call a woman, but I am happy to report that we have evolved beyond false definitions of gender. Your planet is of interest to us because your struggles in the areas of sex and race enable our social scientists to better understand our evolution."

"Then you have a government and legal system somewhat like ours?"

"Heavens, no," she answered much too vehemently and then, to insure that she meant no offense, she added, "there may be some similarities, but it is far more complex and not nearly as dependent on the populace's unthinking acceptance of myths."

"Such as," I asked?

"Your Constitution. Those who wrote it rather clearly did so to protect the existing economic structure including slavery, but Americans believe that the Constitution guarantees freedom and justice equally despite all the contrary experience. Actually, one of your legal writers explained the phenomenon when he wrote: "Those who wield effective control in the nation make, when considered necessary, that amount of social adjustment that will help to siphon off sufficient discontent to enable the societal status quo to be maintained . . . [T]oken or cosmetic gains are extended, [but] no real distribution of wealth, prestige, or social power takes place."[2]

"My goodness. You are citing a good friend, Professor Arthur S. Miller. He died some years ago, but he was part of a small minority of legal scholars who discounted the role of legal doctrine and controlling precedent in our jurisprudence. Most, as he put it, 'parse Supreme Court decisions with an intensity similar to that of Scholastics arguing over the meaning of the ancient texts of Aristotle and Plato.'[3]

"African-American experience confirms Professor Miller's conclusions about how our law works. Not many, though, are willing to speak openly about the functioning of our Constitution and even fewer are willing to listen carefully to efforts at serious critiques that are easily dismissed as subversive."

"It is all very interesting, Professor, but I digress from my primary mission. "I can gauge by your appearance. You are one of those humans who over time have been referred to by your society as 'colored,' 'Negro' and 'black.' We also know that you are one who has studied the matter of race and American law at great length. We have studied your writing with more puzzlement than enlightenment."

"And what don't you understand?" I asked, defensively.

"Well, your knowledge of America's racial history is impressive, but your writings hedge shamelessly about what the future might bring—as though you had learned little from your historical studies. Your writings, moreover, fail to shed much light on the role of civil rights professionals who claim to work for the downtrodden, while, one way or another, they are either directly or indirectly in the employ of those who perpetuate and participate in policies disadvantaging blacks and other minority people."

"In particular, I am here to question you about the real role of what are often called 'affirmative action officers.'"

I was flabbergasted. "Please be seated," I said. "I am at this moment writing a speech for a large group of affirmative action officers. I will help you if I can and perhaps you will share with me how our racial problems, and those of us who work on them, appear from the perspective of your life star."

Accepting my invitation, Chiara sat down on the side of the large stone I had been using as a desk. I had to shield my eyes from the almost blinding glare from the space suit. I thought at first it was the sun's reflection, but realized that much of the dazzling light emanated from the suit itself.

"I am sorry it's so bright, but I cannot remove it in your atmosphere. Still, there is a remedy. Focus your gaze just over my head and try to imagine what I look like."

I did as she said and miraculously she slowly transformed from a shiny, space-suited creature from outer space into a regally beautiful woman with luminous brown skin, and features that conveyed intelligence, serenity, and a uniquely African grace. This woman's countenance conveyed a militance, a readiness to fight that distinguished her from this society's commercialized ideal of beauty. Her clothing was what a warrior on her planet must wear, light in weight but intended to deflect blows and whatever weapons are in use there. Circling her waist, a wide belt held a strange weapon, long like a sword, but able, evidently, to launch the projectiles she carried in a small bag also attached to her belt. Without doubt, she was a very handsome woman, but not one to be trifled with at home, and certainly not while here on her mission.

I stared, mesmerized. She smiled, suggesting firmly, "now, can we continue."

"Is that how you look on your home star?" I asked, trying to sound nonchalant.

She paused, obviously uncertain of how to respond. "I . . . I cannot easily describe how I look at home, but I appear here as a visualization of your imagination. It is intended to ease your discomfort not—as it appears—replace one distraction with another. Perhaps I should transform back to my space suit image?"

"No, no," I said a bit too rapidly, " I am adjusting." Given her psychic powers, I dared not dwell on the matter, but if this brown-skinned Joan of Arc was the product of my imagination, she represented in visual form my belief that black women will ultimately save our people.

"Now," she suggested again, "can we get started."

"One final question." I asked, "If you are able to use my imagination to transform yourself into human form, why do you need to come this great distance to ask questions the answers to which must be easily accessible to you and your scientists?"

She smiled. "Like your Socrates, we believe that enlightenment for the teacher as well as the student is more important than answers and can be gained best through the medium of questions."

I nodded. "Before you offer me enlightenment via your questions, tell me, Chiara. What do your scientists think of those of us who work professionally on civil rights problems?"

Chiara spoke quickly from what seemed an inexhaustible source of knowledge.

"You are an intriguing group. We have determined that there is a gyroscopic effect in the effort by black Americans to achieve racial reform through law. That is, each new barrier in your struggle for racial equality somehow resembles earlier opposition though in a transformed state."

"I am not certain that I am following you," I interjected.

"Please," Chiara insisted, "let me set out our findings first and then we can discuss them." I nodded my assent.

"We wonder whether your scholars recognize what we view as the fallacy in the commonly-held view in your society that the protracted effort by blacks to gain freedom and civil rights in your country constituted a long, unbroken line of slow but steady strides toward equality."

"I have said as much," I acknowledged.

"Good. Then you may also agree that what you denominate as 'progress' is a cyclical phenomenon in which legal rights are gained, then lost, then gained again in response to economic and political developments in the country over which black people exercise little or no control. It appears to us that the law has always been a part of rather than an exception to this cyclical phenomenon. Would you agree?"

I nodded, amazed at her understanding. "What your scientists have observed is not lost on some of us here. In fact, Chiara, I have also used the analogy of a giant, unseen gyroscope, because even our best efforts are unable to divert it permanently from its pre-planned equilibrium requiring dominance for whites over blacks."

"Good, Professor. So you understand that while your racial equality goals evolve and the society even accepts those remedies you civil rights advocates have urged on it, your subordinate status remains unchanged. Its stability is enhanced rather than undermined by the movement up through the class ranks of the precious few who too quickly are deemed to have 'made it'?"

"You have it right, Chiara. I only wish I could get white people who have lived their lives here to gain the sense of race you have observed from afar."

"Then, we are puzzled. Your writing, Professor, seems to reflect the view we are discussing and yet we find there a maddening optimism that pervades its pages leading us to believe that you know more than you have revealed, or that you and other civil rights professionals like you are earning good incomes by pretending that stagnation is progress and that setbacks are somehow gains."

"That last statement," I objected, "is unfair. There are self-servers working in civil rights, but you will find no more there than in any other area of a society."

"Perhaps," Chiara responded, "but by our calculations, the gains your people have made in recent decades have been more symbolic than real—except for the more fortunate ones like you, and even your higher rung on the societal ladder is fragile. Am I right? Meanwhile, great numbers of black people are worse off now than at any time since slavery. What you hailed as a great victory two generations ago, *Brown v. Board of Education*,[4] has failed either to bring equal educational opportunity in the public schools, its asserted mission, or establish an unshakable standard of racial equality in your fundamental law, its original goal.

"Professor, our observers have been impressed by your annual celebrations of the *Brown* decision. Each year they become more moving, but we have searched without success for another legal precedent that your society is increasingly willing to commemorate, and less and less willing to follow."

"Chiara, I admit that much of your assessment about the status of black people is accurate. It illustrates all too well my sense that you understand us far better than we understand ourselves. As an advanced society, I hope you will tell us what we should do to break what I call this gyroscopic cycle that, no matter what we do, maintains blacks always in a subordinate role."

"I will not because I cannot," Chiara said, shaking her head. "The pieces of your puzzle are not in place. There is much we cannot determine."

"For example?" I asked.

"For example, the hostile response to the affirmative action remedies put forth to cure the effects of long-standing racist practices. Why do whites react with such hostility to these programs even when they benefit as much and often more than blacks from their operation?"

"I suspect they do not know themselves.

Opposition to any policy that appears aimed at easing the subordinate status of blacks is as automatic as it is hostile. Professor Miller put it well when he wrote: "Many white Americans, obviously with exceptions, simply are not willing to assimilate people of color into the mainstream of society. The result is a de facto caste system, with the majority of blacks becoming ever more permanent segments of the underclass in America."[5]

Chiara nodded in agreement. "It is not as though the test scores and other so-called 'neutral' standards in use actually select the best candidate. Available studies show that these pen and paper tests actually measure past opportunity better than future potential.[6] So, why are so many whites willing to accept measures that disadvantage most of them?"

"A question much easier to ask than answer. Those working-class whites who are most disadvantaged by college admissions tests, for example, are simply not rational on this subject. They seem totally resistive to giving up any of what they consider their racial prerogatives, but they are far more accepting of the class disadvantage they suffer throughout their lives."

Chiara started to speak, but I added, "There is another facet of the problem. It's the wholly cynical policy of whites in the leadership classes who claim adherence to affirmative action policies, but explain their failure to implement them fully on the lack of qualified minorities when they know that the qualifications they insist on are precisely the credentials and skills that have been long denied to people of color. Those qualifications are often irrelevant or of little importance to the effective accomplishment of the positions for which they serve as barriers to most blacks and other minorities.

"So, you see, Chiara, I concede the basic accuracy of your analysis."

"Well, I can understand the psychic benefits whites think they get from opposing black gains, even when they are actually hurting themselves. What I can't comprehend is the role of so many blacks who have achieved a measure of success in your society. Why would they accept affirmative action positions when they know their numbers are limited, not by their talents, but by the number the school or business is willing to accept as a kind of legal insulation against justified charges of racism?"

"I think most black leaders challenge the racial status quo. I think when we get positions as the first black whatever, we feel that by our performance we will break down resistance to hiring more minorities. Our methods differ, but the goal of gaining equal opportunity is the same for most."

"Professor, how can you say that? You understand that virtually every gain you get comes only when whites get more, and yet you hail such gains as proof that 'you shall overcome.' It would be sad enough if you were simply running the people you lead around in a circle. But you are losing ground and losing people. Your young men have no work and are increasingly earning not an income, but long terms in prison. Your young women are becoming mothers before their time. 'Children having children' is how one of your leaders put it. These statistics are worsening while you worry about defending an affirmative action that basically protects more whites than it offers opportunity to blacks and other people of color."

I was startled by her vehemence. She noticed. "I am sorry, but your behavior is a greater mystery than the white people wanting to keep the benefits of their

51

whiteness. We simply don't understand. I am not able to give you my message without understanding why you keep on quietly pushing for rights in a system where your people are dying or facing lives that are close to living death."

"What are you asking, Chiara? Would we be better off if we urged our people to pick up arms and kill as many white people as possible before we all are killed?"

"I know you believe in nonviolence. James Weldon Johnson, one of your great political and artistic leaders, warned that it would be futile for blacks to turn to violence. But out of their frustration and despair, many of your people are turning to violence, though mostly against one another. And many more are doing violence to themselves. They spend what they don't have on luxuries they don't need, listen to music that is pornographic, patronize films that revel in the worse form of racial stereotypes, and generally act as though their lives are worthless to others and to themselves. I am not telling you anything you don't know. You must care what is happening all around you."

"I care. Many of us care." For a long moment, I sat silently and became aware again of the solitude of the place, its isolation from the world Chiara was describing. She sat opposite me, quiet, a portrait of patience.

"Chiara, people do what they can do. As you certainly know, I have no influence with the blacks you are describing. It is even hard to influence many of those who have escaped the despair of the ghetto. There will be blacks who return from prison angry enough to do what revolutionaries in other societies have done, take up arms, become terrorists. Our failure, I know, will spawn the bloody violence of open revolt."

"Professor, I am not getting through to you. What I have been describing is violent and bloody. And, if I may say it, your resistance as shown by civil rights peoples' vigorous efforts to win law suits, influence legislation, and engage in peaceful protests, seems to us more like resignation. It is certainly not relevant to these lives placed on self-destruct.

Chiara waited for me to answer her. When I didn't, she implored, "You don't have to resort to violence. Dr. King, a major prophet of your people, proved that you can advance your cause by organizing massive protests and boycotts."

"What you suggest, Chiara, is easier said than done. King's peaceful protests worked because the nation, having become the world's leader, was embarrassed by Jim Crow signs. It was ready to move away from overtly racist practices. Civil rights demonstrations helped push out the old policy and make way for changes that, as you say, helped some of us while pushing the rest deeper into a poverty that does not appear to be based on race.

"It's much more complicated than you think, Chiara. Perhaps your people understand American racism less well than you assume. Leadership is tough for everyone in America. Ask the president or any elected official trying to get people to act in their own interest.

"But if you want to find out why we are not rebelling against racism instead of trying to defend affirmative action, Chiara, let me give you the best answer I can. Despite your criticism, I think there are many blacks, other people of color, and some whites who are committed to the cause of racial justice. But all of us have allowed ourselves to be a part of the racial pattern of subordination in this country in the hope—often vain—that our service would somehow make things better, rather than worse. And, in this, we adhere to a long tradition.

"Slaves fought in the Revolutionary War, for both America and the British, based on promises that by their participation, they and their families might gain freedom. Some did, many did not.

"Frederick Douglass lobbied continuously to have blacks accepted into military service during the Civil War, and in the same hope. And toward the end of the war, some slaves responded to the call to fight on the side of the Confederacy in return for promises of freedom. In every war since then, blacks have fought abroad for freedoms that were denied them at home, both before they left and after they returned.

"Consider as well, civil rights lawyers who over the last several decades have utilized the courts to change legal patterns of discrimination that have often benefitted whites more than most blacks. Those rights have provided a stability and a legitimacy to a still racist society that could not have been brought about without their efforts. Their intentions—and those of the clients they served—were to bring racial equality to the law, not provide justifications for the continued exclusion of people of color. In fact, they did both. Why is their work not a mystery to your scientists? I could continue, but you certainly see my point."

"I see, and can understand how your leaders at an earlier time could seek equality by deeds, by efforts to change the law, but given what you know and the dire plight of your people, I do not understand why you continue a struggle that transforms your freedom campaigns into new and ever-more effective fetters."

"If your people can provide us with a more effective strategy," I replied, "I am certain that our leaders would welcome it. You see, Chiara, many of us are only now coming to see that our real enemy is not ignorance about race or bigoted people. Of course, some racial hostility is unthinking bigotry, but much more is built on the perception that black gains threaten the main component of status for many whites: the sense that as whites, they are entitled to priority and preference over blacks. The law has mostly encouraged and upheld what Mr. Plessy argued in *Plessy v. Ferguson* was a property right in whiteness, and those at the top of the society have increased their profits and their power, because the masses of whites were too occupied in keeping blacks down to note the large gap between their status and that of whites on top.

"At the beginning of the nation's history, slavery served this stabilizing function. Back in 1832, when the Virginia legislature convened to consider ending slavery in the wake of Nat Turner's South Hampton revolt, Thomas Roderick Dew argued that despite its economic limitations via capital/wage-labor, (and presumably its dangers) slavery (should be retained he argued because it) afforded an ideological basis to resolve conflict between propertied and unpropertied whites with the Negro as low-man on the totem pole. And thus, slavery was consistent with the spirit of republicanism in its ability to promote freedom and community among whites.

"Slavery is ended, but blacks continue to serve the role of buffers between those most advantaged in the society, and those whites seemingly content to live the lives of the rich and famous through the pages of the tabloids and television soap operas. For the fact is that the general belief as to which race is dominant in the society has helped motivate—and

55

justify—the many compromises in which the interests of blacks are bartered and sometimes sacrificed to further accords between groups of whites.

"The Supreme Court rejected the 'separate but equal' doctrine of *Plessy v. Ferguson*[7] more than four decades ago, but today the passwords for gaining judicial recognition of the still viable property right to the advantages of being white in a society that for generations has discriminated against those who are not white include 'higher entrance scores,'[8] 'seniority,'[9] and 'neighborhood schools.'[10] Hypocrisy remains the keystone of this continuing injustice as indicated by the reassertion of Justice Harlan's ringing—if unrealistic—assertion that our Constitution is color blind, now the major argument of those who oppose all affirmative action remedies.

"Often, white opposition is not rational.[11] But it provides more than ample proof that a property value in whiteness exists and unless infringements are carefully tailored, it will gain judicial protection that frustrates the efforts of civil rights lawyers seeking to translate formally recognized rights into substantive entitlement essential to the meaningful remediation of past (and continuing) racial disadvantage."

"Are these not discouraging developments?" Chiara asked. "Are your efforts not hopeless?"

"Struggle for what you think is right against what you know is wrong is never hopeless, Chiara."

"It is a fine statement for you." Chiara said softly. "You can do your work in these beautiful surroundings reached in that nice car parked below on the road. But what can your philosophy of struggle for struggle's sake possibly mean to the growing number of your people who are sliding further and further into poverty and despair? To them your noble statement must sound empty, meaningless. You will simply have to become more militant, more willing to take action. Violent or not, it will be threatening to your enemies and they will retaliate. But it is the only way. Professor, it is time to wake the nation and . . . " Her voice trailed off.

Suddenly, I realized what was bothering her. "Could it be, Chiara, that on your life star, you are the counterpart of our civil rights leaders, that you were chosen for this mission because of your color, and that you seek here to convince us to undertake the militant, even violent, action here you are unable to get your people to do there?"

Chiara looked shocked. "You are closer than you realize to a truth you cannot possibly understand," she said firmly. And, as she spoke, she dissolved before my eyes to be replaced by a space-suited being at least ten feet tall and as fearsome as Chiara had been beautiful.

At sight of this new figure, I did not try to control my impulse to run, but the being—evidently sensing that impulse—froze me where I stood with the wave of an arm.

"Well, Earth Professor, we have learned enough about the motivations for your civil rights workers to better address any such tendencies among those like yourselves on our planet."

"Are you Chiara?" I asked.

The being laughed. "Let us say simply that we employ Chiara to assist us in what you call civil rights work. In this instance, she has done her work—and ours—quite well.

"Goodbye, Earth Professor."

An hour later, I was still standing in the same spot—unable to move. The sun was going down and cast a multicolored light across the landscape. I struggled and was able after a while to move, first a finger, then a hand, and after several minutes, an arm.

Slowly, I regained the use of my body. I started to gather my papers that had scattered across the small clearing. Perhaps it was all a bad dream, I rationalized. Or, even if it happened, what damage could come from my statements? I began to feel better, and then I found it—a parchment scroll inside a metallic cylinder like those Chiara carried in her belt. I opened it quickly. It was dated that very day.

Dear Earth Professor,

I beg your forgiveness. It was not my intention that you should suffer for befriending a stranger. I had to do what I did, but I learned much that will help me and those I represent.

Please. You must know that there is no physical gyroscope preset to keep people of color subordinated to people who are white. But neither is there a law that will respond with justice simply because your legal analysis is sound and your cause is worthy. Both the gyroscope and the law are representations, facsimiles of your society that are the motivating force of their movement even as both seem to operate by an internal energy source.

Your nation is structured to support the powerful and suppress the powerless. The law will seldom deviate from this pattern. On occasion, it may anticipate societal reform and seem even to lead or command change. But it remains a representation, and will not stray too far from the pattern set by the society.

Those involved in civil rights must continue their work with increased militancy for, as one of your Earth's early prophets said: "Faith, if it has no works, is dead, being alone." But with faith, work, and understanding, there is much to be done—by all of us who struggle against the prejudice of caste and color.

Extraterrestrially yours,

Chiara

The Citadel

Service in the cause of truth and justice is no less worthy of praise because it is misunderstood, misused, or condemned.

"**F**riend, have you talked to a psychiatrist about your attraction to strong women? And," Geneva was smiling, "you seem to meet them in the strangest places."

"Cut out the zingers, Geneva. I noticed you did not seem very surprised as I described Chiara, a really remarkable woman who—wait a minute. Geneva. Please! Don't tell me that you were Chiara. You really should stop."

Geneva couldn't help laughing. "If you insist, I won't tell you whether or not I was Chiara. You seem to admire her. I don't know why. She's a lot more critical of you and your civil rights friends than I am. She did have a point, though, namely that you who are concerned about the future of blacks don't have forever to simply worry about what will happen next."

"I know that," I responded, still miffed that Geneva might have been Chiara, but given how I had gone for the ruse—if that's what it was—too embarrassed to insist on the truth. It is not easy to maintain a relationship with Geneva, given her awesome powers. Thank heavens, ours is based on love and respect—not what my envious male friends assume.

Geneva interrupted my thoughts. "Hello, friend. Are you with me. We don't have forever to get these stories together."

"Risky though it is, I'm still thinking about Chiara, wondering whether her mission was undertaken on behalf of those in power or those seeking relief from oppression."

"It might be for both. That could explain her particular interest in affirmative action officers. They often work for institutions whose racial policies leave much to be desired and trying to further the interests of blacks both in and out of the organization. It's almost impossible to please both the company you are working for and the blacks you are trying to help. Often, these individuals find they don't have the trust of either."

"And, I can tell you from my experience, you are not even sure that the course you decide on is the best or even a good way to help the civil rights cause."

Geneva agreed. "Strength of commitment does not guarantee perfect insight into the effect of our actions. Our most unselfish work may turn out to do harm as great as the injustices we tried to end. That knowledge provides a troubling counter-theme that is present even as we receive recognition for confronting some of the evils we encounter. This troubling counter-theme, we might call it the difficulty of doing good, is the message in the next Afrolantica Legacy. If you're ready, I'll begin."

clocloclo

From a distance, the Citadel resembles Camelot. Located high on an impressive mountain, the Citadel is often invisible in the mists and clouds that abound at such altitudes. But on a sunny day, particularly after rains have cleansed the atmosphere, it is both visible and awe-inspiring. Its high battlements of white stone reflect the sunlight so brilliantly that it is difficult to tell whether the sun or the Citadel is the source of light.

Much after the event, those who claim to have

been witnesses, explained that though it was night, an unusually bright moon illuminated the Citadel, enabling them to witness the strange events. From a conflicting melange of stories, these facts emerged. At some point during the midnight hour, two hooded figures appeared at the edge of the tallest parapet and with minimal ceremony eased a large, oblong sack over the wall. Other hooded figures then appeared alongside them. Some hurled stones after the sack. One tossed bouquets of flowers. As in slow motion, the sack, the stones, and the flowers drifted slowly down to the ground beneath the great walls. After a few moments, the sack began to move, and what appeared from a distance to be a person emerged and, with the assistance of others who seemed to have expected this strange arrival, moved out of the line of stones and flowers that continued to fall.

Long ago, the lowlanders, as the people are known who live on the rolling plains that stretch out below the Citadel and extend far beyond the horizon, had become accustomed to the vagaries of those who ruled from the Citadel. Even so, those who gathered to trade tales of what they termed the midnight bag sacrifice were unable to agree on its meaning. None of them, though, were greatly troubled by the strange event. There was, they had decided, little purpose to wondering about what they could neither understand nor change. Besides, they had grown used to enduring—enduring the burdens of their work, its unfairness, and its likely permanence. The lowlanders labored in the fields or factories where work is hard, hours are long, and wages are hardly sufficient to provide the shelter and sustenance that enable them to continue in the jobs that dominate their lives.

For countless generations, those in the Citadel

have ruled the domain that spreads beyond their mountain and includes the lowlands. The Citadel's current residents govern with greater benevolence than did their ancestors who overran the lowlanders' country hundreds of years before. Even so, they expect as their due the obedience of the lowlanders who perform the strenuous physical labor necessary for the Citadel's prosperity. Despite their hard work, the lowlanders are neither invited to participate in the Citadel's ruling Council of Elders, nor allowed a claim to the wealth that they help produce but cannot enjoy. Even the lowlanders' most restrained requests for their fair share of the benefits of their labors are rejected.

Perhaps more clearly than the challengers, the guardians of the Citadel's power understand that any real reform would forever change the mountaintop kingdom. This, of course, they are determined to resist. Those in power understand the need for eternal vigilance, and to this task, involving endless intrigue and deception, they willingly devote their lives. They seem not to recognize the larger burden of their power: a gnawing insecurity—precisely that disquieting unease the acquisition of power was supposed to vanquish.

It should be known, though, that the lowlanders were not always resigned to events beyond their control. Their ancestors had mounted periodic challenges to the Citadel. Quite a few among the living could still recall the events of some dozens of years ago, and repeated the saga to all those who would listen.

A popular lowlander leader had disappeared under suspicious circumstances following a secret negotiation session with Citadel officials. The disappearance, shrouded in secrecy and denial, sparked a great upheaval among the lowlanders. Many of them spoke out, protested, and, when all else failed, even took up arms. This group made a strong and insistent demand for representation at the governing level of the Citadel. Those who took up the fight did so in the face of great hostility and very real danger. The Citadel's swift and ruthless retaliation caused uncounted thousands to suffer economic ruin, or to fear it. Thousands more endured the perils of arrest and imprisonment at the hands of lowlander officials in the employ of the Citadel who, viewing the insurgents as ingrates, subversives, and traitors, treated them accordingly. Even ordinary lowlanders, those who would have benefitted from a successful revolt, were ambivalent about the wisdom of revolutionary actions that brought down the Citadel's wrath upon them all. None could deny, though, that the struggle contributed to a sense of instability in the land—one that even the Citadel's top rulers could not ignore.

At the time of what is remembered as the Great Revolt, Xercis was Protector of the Citadel, its top leader. At that time, he had only recently inherited his position from his father in a line of succession that stretched back beyond the memory of any now living. From birth, he had been trained for the position he had held for three decades with a dedication that knew no limit. Indeed, Xercis tended the Citadel's great traditions with all the fierce devotion of a high priest in some ancient temple. Even his detractors acknowledged that his stewardship was without parallel.

Xercis had considered his father's rule overly harsh, condemning the lowlanders to virtual serfdom. Accordingly, soon after he was named Protector, he eased the most onerous taxes his father had levied upon the lowlanders working in factories and on small farms. But with the current unrest, he had to concede that his well-intended actions were a mistake. Thoroughly downtrodden peoples exhaust themselves with the tasks of survival. It is when their conditions improve, however slightly, that some among them envision a better life and, nurturing dreams of freedom, sow the seeds of eventual revolt.

Even now, the lowlanders' were resenting and resisting laws promulgated by the Citadel that were humane by comparison with those issued at earlier times. This unrest, slight as it still was, worried the Citadel's leaders. They would have worried even more had they known that there dwelt within the Citadel, within their Protector's very household, one who was sympathetic to the lowlanders. This was Tamar, Xercis' daughter and only child. Tamar's mother had died in childbirth. Xercis had devoted himself to Tamar's education. She had a keen mind, and at an early age exhibited a remarkable grasp of the complex doctrines and arcane language of the Citadel's government. He gave her both his wide knowledge and a strong independence of mind. He was proud of the first, but came to be ambivalent about the second.

Tamar viewed the protesting lowlanders with a fresh eye. She had worked with them in their hospitals and taught in their schools. She believed that they should not be put down as traitors; rather that they should be treated as equals. Xercis' early difficulties with reform occurred, she believed, because his reforms had not gone far enough. But Tamar was devoted to her father and for a long time, kept her ideas to herself. Then, the Citadel's harsh reaction to the early stages of the lowlanders' current protests moved her to speak out.

"Are their demands," she finally burst out, "so

unreasonable? Their labor and their skills are the source of the Citadel's wealth, its strength. Is it fair—is it wise—to deny them a voice in what their labor makes possible?"

Xercis was speechless. Maintaining power was the Citadel's central duty. Could it be that Tamar, while having the intellect, skill, and courage to rule, lacked the devotion to authority and tradition so vital to the Citadel's effective governance? For the future, a barrier loomed, one that threatened a quiet transition of power when Xercis died or stepped down.

Xercis and Tamar had many heated arguments about the Citadel's treatment of the lowlanders. "You are young and head-strong, Tamar," Xercis told her. "Reserve your conclusions until you are older and have more experience. Our treatment of the lowlanders is firm, but not brutal, rigid but not inappropriate."

"Much as I respect your wisdom, father," she responded, "it does not moderate the Citadel's harsh rules. It does not relieve the lowlanders. Real reform is needed. And, without it," she paused, "turmoil is inevitable."

"Tamar," Xercis spoke sternly, "the price of maintaining power over others is the continuing risk of their revolt. But we must abide by the teaching of our forebears. Whatever its cost, we must maintain dominance. An alternative to our power, gained through revolt might well beget less justice rather than more." Tamar opened her mouth to respond, but Xercis would not be interrupted. "Because of your work among the lowlanders, my daughter, you have changed. No longer the missionary from the Citadel to them, you are increasingly their advocate against the Citadel."

Tamar was moved by the deep hurt and frustration in her father's voice. "I am a missionary for all, seeking rights and justice for all," she responded quietly.

Xercis looked at his daughter and slowly shook his head. "Those are only words, my child. Your quest for the unreal imperils your chance to become the Citadel's first woman Protector. In this position, you would see more clearly the limits as well as the potential of your crusades."

"But father . . . "

Xercis interrupted, unable to bear her attitude. He spoke with finality. "You, Tamar, must decide whether you will carry on the traditions of our hallowed forebears or those of a race who were their traditional enemies. But Tamar, know, as you weigh your decision, that the Citadel is and must remain opposed to granting equality to the lowlanders."

Xercis, as Protector, ruled the Citadel's extended domain. By tradition, he sought guidance and concurrence from the Council of Elders. The elders were a small, select group who, along with the Protector's family, constituted the Citadel's leaders. Admission to the Council was limited to the most gifted children of Council members and other leaders, all of whom were outstanding graduates of an elite preparatory school. A certain number of these graduates were chosen to become apprentices to Council Elders, and some of this group were later sponsored by an Elder for beginning leadership roles. These procedures led to the selection of Elders, some able and others not. All were, not remarkably, almost identical in background, education, and opinion. All were male. No woman had ever been considered for these roles. Indeed, most of the Elders were finding it hard to imagine a woman on the Council, much less as Protector, even one as accomplished as Tamar, their own Protector's daughter.

Even more far-fetched was the notion that a low-lander could be present in the Council's sessions, let alone speak or cast a vote as a Council member. Yet exactly that was what the lowlanders were now demanding. Having never sat in the ruling Council, the lowlanders assumed that their voices and votes would ensure that their interests would be represented and accommodated. And to achieve that aim, they were engaging in an array of nonviolent protests, sit-down strikes, disruptive marches, and roadside blockades.

Upon first hearing the lowlanders' demand for representation, Xercis and the Council of Elders summarily rejected it. Lowlanders, possessing none of the traditional traits that were prerequisites for admission, were not fitted to make serious decisions affecting the well-being of untold thousands. This answer Xercis communicated to the lowlanders' leaders; he expected that they would accept it, see reason, and subside. But Xercis' answer only infuriated the lowlanders and led thousands more to join the ranks of the protesters. Within a week, they gathered at the bottom of the Citadel mountain, surrounded it, and refused to allow anyone to pass through their unarmed but determined ranks.

Xercis and the Council met to consider how to send the lowlanders back to work and to restore order. The Citadel had superior arms, and some Elders urged that the revolt be put down by force. But other Elders suspected—as many a repressive regime has found out to its cost—that the resort to force to quell a peaceful protest might only heighten the rebels' fervor. These Elders counseled patience, predicting that the rebels would tire of their blockade and return to the relative comfort of their homes. All looked to Xercis for his decision.

Tamar, though not eligible to attend the critical meeting of the Council of Elders, made clear to her father whose side she was on.

"But you do not understand," Xercis had protested to his daughter. "It is not merely that the lowlanders are a different people. Our method of choosing leaders provides the Citadel with stability based on the recognition of ability and the reward of achievement." Xercis could not keep the irritation out of his voice.

Tamar looked across the great table in his chambers and smiled at him. "And the apprentices, those from whom the elders are chosen, how are they selected?" she asked. It was a question to which they both knew the answer. "Suppose, father, that we allowed those who were unrelated or unconnected to the elders, to serve in these positions? Suppose, even, that we searched across the land for our apprentices?"

"Daughter," again exasperation sharpened his voice, "I am no love-smitten prince chasing across the land looking for a Cinderella whose foot will fit a glass slipper. What you suggest would simply raise hopes that would be cruelly dashed. You know as well as I about the gap in schooling, the great differences in culture."

"All true," Tamar acknowledged, "but merit, father, is out there. New blood. Intelligent, if less well-schooled. Courageous, if not as attuned to our patrician tastes. There are men and women out there who could breathe new life into our dusty halls. And," she added warningly, "give new hope to the lowlanders. Their rage is growing. They will not abandon their blockade, and those who would break their peaceful protest with violence will play into the rebels' hands."

Xercis sighed. How had he, the very soul of moderation, come to have such a daughter, one who seemed bent on challenging his authority?

The Council of Elders debated long and passionately about how to resolve the lowlanders' revolt. Finally, it was Xercis', moment to speak. As he moved from his chair to the center of the podium, he looked suddenly old, weighed by his 60 years.

"I am drawn to both sides of this debate. To you who advocate a response with arms—but fear that a victory bought with great bloodshed will surely foment even more fierce revolt; to you who urge patience —but inaction can be seen as weakness and will only encourage the rebels." He paused, then went on. "In this dilemma, I suggest a third course."

"Let us tell the lowlanders that we have always intended one day to provide them with representation at the Citadel. That this day has now come. That we will open up the Citadel to them." As the Elders started to mutter angrily, Xercis raised his hand for silence. "At the same time, we must warn them that their presence here"—he looked around the great Council chamber—"will meet with resistance from some members of the Citadel and from some lowlanders as well. Thus, change must be gradual, building support and acceptance as it proceeds." He paused.

Many among the Council thought that Xercis had suffered a serious attack of senility. For the first time in Xercis' rule, the Elders interrupted him and openly questioned his decision. "Admitting a lowlander," one cried, "is surrender." Added another: "Surrender, yes, but without its dignity!" Two or three Elders discerned the outlines of Xercis' strategy. "Allow him to finish," they interjected. "We must not forget that the most potent weapon in the arsenal of power is not brute force, but guile."

"We can in one action," Xercis went on, "assuage the rage of the lowlanders while making it appear that fate, rather than ourselves, is the source of the conditions about which they complain. By admitting a few of them slowly, we will appear fair and open-minded. We will win the allegiance of those who enter the Citadel, and quell the complaints of those who say we exclude lowlanders from our ranks. Those who join us will praise the qualities that earned their entry to the Citadel. Those who remain outside will blame the personal shortcomings that keep them below. Most lowlanders, meanwhile, if they respond as they have in the past, will blame their exclusion from the Citadel on the radicals among them who foment distrust with demands for preferential treat-ment and percentages of representation. The major-ity will not join the revolt.

"We will win," Xercis concluded, "by admitting the error of our past policies. Only by ostensibly renouncing them, will we ensure their continued via-bility." Though he did not mention her name, Xercis realized that he had learned something from Tamar— though perhaps not the lesson she most wished to convey. After long and often bitter debate, Xercis gained the Council's approval for his plan. The Citadel would admit one lowlander to the Council, provided the individual was of their choosing.

The host of lowlanders moved the line of their blockade close to the Citadel's walls. They expected that their clamor for social reform and representation would bring the Citadel's rulers rushing to the ram-parts. Instead, the gates swung open, the Citadel's leaders came forth and called for a small delegation of lowlanders to meet with them.

Xercis was distressed but not surprised to see Tamar in the lowlanders' delegation. She had quietly left the Citadel some weeks before, leaving only a sealed letter for him. "Dear Father, I have decided to work for the Citadel's future among the least of its peoples. Living close to them, I will be able to assess their needs and evaluate how the Citadel's rulers can best respond to them. I realize that my absence can jeopardize my chances of succeeding you, and may even provide an opportunity for my opponents to expel me from the Citadel. I accept these risks. I will always consider the Citadel my home, and I will always deserve my place there." As she predicted, many of the Citadel's Elders did deem his daughter's desertion an act of treason. Her departure was a heavy blow to Xercis, and now he did not greet her.

As Tamar stepped forward to speak for the lowlanders, Xercis raised his hand. "Let me speak, Tamar. When you have heard the Council's decision in this matter, we will hear from you." His voice rang out, stilling the crowd. "For years we—the Elders and I—have allowed no lowlander to serve in the Council of Elders. Now, you have made us realize that this is intolerable. We have come to understand that you should be a part of the Citadel, and we are prepared to welcome you. But in all of our best interests, we must lay down guidelines for this historic transition."

His words stunned the crowd into silence, as he continued. "Governing our vast domain is a difficult and exacting task. Not everyone is able to rise to its demands, and we must not, as a nation, risk elevating anyone who lacks the skill and wisdom to do so. Therefore, we will admit to the Citadel only those lowlanders who meet our time-honored qualifications."

The delegation conferred. To most of them, it seemed an honor to have admission to the Council be based on merit. With great solemnity and joy, they accepted Xercis' proposal. After agreeing that an open competition would be held on a set date, the delegation promised to suspend the blockade. As they left the Citadel, every lowlander in the delegation believed that its walls had moved, if only a little. So Tamar believed as well, and she returned to the Citadel with her father.

In the weeks following the Citadel's offer, the lowlanders diligently prepared for the competition that would grant one of them a seat on the Council of Elders. The aspirants were to respond orally to a series of questions designed to test their leadership ability. Xercis and the Elders would evaluate their answers and choose the most impressive person to fill the first available seat on the Council of Elders.

As they listened to the competing lowlanders, the Elders were wary. Although they had agreed to the competition, they had not accepted that any lowlander would be their equal. Although many of the competitors answered correctly the complex questions the Elders had labored to devise, the expertise of one young man amazed them. Indeed, this Timur demolished most of their serious reservations about admitting a lowlander. Even when his answers were identical to the other contestants, he still outshone them.

He also had, for a lowlander, a distinguished pedigree, and his family had managed to accumulate an unusual amount of wealth. With it, they had invested the money in Timur's future, sending him to a superior school in another land, a school that, unlike the best schools in their kingdom, admitted lowlanders. There, Timur had excelled, and cultivated many of the qualities shared by those in the Citadel. He understood several, now-unused languages which allowed him to study obscure historical texts. He also had joined exclusive fraternities, known for their allegiance to pursuing "the best in life." Many of the friends he made, the children of the elite in other kingdoms, spoke highly of him to their counterparts in the Citadel. You could almost forget, they noted in praise, that Timur was a lowlander.

In addition, Timur was different in his manner from the other lowlander competitors. He lacked the brash, assertive tone of those who resented their long exclusion from the Citadel. Nor was he timid, like the lowlanders who had been unable to develop self-confidence after years of being ignored, dismissed, and placed in jobs below their abilities. Timur answered all questions confidently but respectfully—even cheerfully. Thus, finding the delicate balance admired by the Elders, he did not appear threatening. If they closed their eyes and heard only his soft voice, they might think he was one of themselves.

Xercis observed the Elders nod in approval when Timur spoke. The other competing lowlanders noticed as well. Some grew angry and openly challenged the Elders—an obvious mistake. Others, thoroughly flustered, misspoke when called upon.

At the close of the competition, the winner was clear to all. Xercis made the announcement: "We have seen today that a break in our hallowed traditions need not invite disaster. Timur has done well for himself. He is truly a credit to his race and should be accepted as their representative into the Council of Elders. I so move." The vote was unanimous. Even those who had harbored misgivings accepted Timur without reservation.

Xercis continued: "I must also add that we owe much of today's events to my daughter, Tamar." And to allay the concern and resentment Tamar had caused by taking on the lowlanders' cause, he said:

"Tamar's willingness to go out among the people, to observe their distress, and to recognize their potential moved us to this event and convinced us that our beloved Citadel will be able to adapt to the challenges of the future, as we and our predecessors have met them in the past."

Tamar was overjoyed to see Timur installed in the Citadel. She had met him years before, recognized him as a likely leader, and—for a time—saw in him something more. Tall and lithe, he had a handsome chiseled face and long, flowing hair. In addition, he seemed determined to help his people in their struggle against the Citadel's oppression. It was only natural that Tamar took it upon herself to introduce Timur to the Citadel. She made sure that he understood all of its unspoken rules, and that he made no mistakes that would mar his performance as the first lowlander to enter the Citadel.

Their friendship blossomed, but Tamar was troubled. Did she resist romance because Timur, for all his talents and education, was a lowlander and not of her heritage? She hoped not. Still, increasingly, she and Timur seemed to be operating on different tracks, ones not necessarily parallel. Her concerns were, in time, destined to grow into fear and misgiving.

At first, Timur sat quietly during the Council meetings, absorbing everything he heard and saw. Of course, the Elders did not want him to assert himself. But if he did, he was but one voice and one vote, and they could safely ignore whatever he said. But then one day Timur did speak up, and the Elders were delighted to find that his views meshed almost exactly with their own. No one was more eloquent than Timur in urging that the harshest steps be taken to stamp out any further revolt among the lowlanders.

Not privy to these secret meetings, the lowlanders could only watch the Citadel from the distance. They had claimed victory when Timur joined the Citadel. And now they waited to see how the representative for whom they had risked so much would relieve the misery of their lives. Over time, a few other lowlanders were admitted, but the Council found their accomplishments crude and unpolished in comparison with their own. Their intentions were good, but they had almost no influence with the Council. Timur had opposed them as unqualified and, in his effort to become a true Citadelian, treated them as badly as any of the Elders.

The lowlanders began to question the Elders' good faith. With much respect, they petitioned the Citadel rulers to admit more of them to its ranks, or from the ranks of other disadvantaged peoples who had joined their struggles over the years. A goodly number of these residents had, in the intervening years, gone to school and worked, gaining experiences that would equip them to serve in the Council of Elders.

Few of the Citadel's rulers were moved by these requests. Besides, lulled by the relative peacefulness following Timur's admission, and the civility of the lowlanders' new demands, the Elders felt confident that they need make no further concessions. Even so, having learned a lesson, when the lowlanders requested a meeting, the Council did not wait this time for the lowlanders to rush the gates, but invited their representatives to a meeting to discuss their concerns. The lowlanders spoke first, their arguments carefully drafted in the language used by the members of the Citadel. Appealing to both law and justice, they argued that proportional representation of fifty percent lowlanders would benefit both groups.

The Council responded diplomatically, giving the answer Xercis had foreseen during their last encounter with the lowlanders. Xercis calmed their visitors by claiming to share their concerns. He regretted, he said, that a most serious and wide-ranging search had turned up no other lowlanders who merited entry. Pointing to the lowlander members, he reminded the lowlander outsiders that the Citadel had demonstrated its commitment to reform. "It would be wrong," Xercis concluded, "to measure our reform by numerical gauges rather than the sincerity by which we have come so far in our mutual quest for reform." Some of the lowlanders—particularly those already inside—were reassured by Xercis; or, like Timur, agreed with him. Others among them recalled their history and their still, subordinated lives. They wondered if they hadn't made a terrible mistake in striking a deal with Xercis.

In the years that followed, the Citadel continued to add lowlander members to its ranks—always one at a time—and usually after one of the older lowlanders died, retired, or moved elsewhere. Each of them resembled Timur more than any of the less-privileged lowlanders who had participated in the Great Revolt. Every so often, a delegation would come from the valley to question the slow pace of progress, and each time it would be greeted civilly by the Citadel's leaders. The discussion always proceeded on much the same terms. Then the delegation would depart, some of its members angry and some reassured—but nothing would have changed.

Tamar also watched and waited for change. She, too, had been confident that Timur's entry into the Citadel, and the admission of colleagues very much like him, would change the Citadel. But she finally had to recognize her mistake in thinking that the

Citadel and her father would share their power so easily.

Tamar finally confronted Timur. "Have you forgotten that you were brought here to satisfy the aspirations of your people, and to represent them here in the halls of power?"

Timur did not try to conceal his arrogance and disdain. "I am here because I won the competition, and I deserved to win it. I owe nothing to you or to anyone else. As an Elder, I have heard the lowlanders' delegation and its pleas for justice. I must tell you that I find them misguided, ill-advised, and hopeless. No one here—myself included—will ever support their petitions. The lowlanders do not need justice. They do not need handouts. What they need is more discipline. With hard work and dedication, they can achieve what I have in my own life."

Tamar simply stared at this man—this stranger, her enemy. This man who, but for the color of his skin, was indistinguishable from any of the Elders—in his manner, his thoughts, and in his very being. And it was she who had brought him into the Citadel. Timur was her responsibility.

The fear in Timur's eyes when she pulled the long knife from her jacket was sweet revenge. She maneuvered him against the wall and raised the knife to his throat. Her voice was colder than the stone he cringed against. "What I threaten today your people will accomplish when they find you out. And, Timur, they will find you out." Then Tamar called for the guards. "Take me away," she said, calm now. "I have attacked and threatened to kill a member of the Council of Elders."

Because few in the Citadel ever betrayed their roles, there had been little need for the sacrifice of the sack, a humiliating form of banishment. In the last

Council meeting he presided over alone, Xercis struggled between his devotion to the Citadel's laws and his love for his daughter. In the end, the Council of Elders rejected his pleas on Tamar's behalf. Unanimously—by the vote of all the Elders, including Timur—Tamar was condemned. The Council then impelled Xercis into selecting Timur, now the consummate insider-outsider, as his successor and thus his assistant in the banishment ritual whereby Tamar would be encased in a canvas sack and lowered from the Citadel's battlements.

Tamar accepted her fate, even welcomed it. She would miss her father, but she did not regret her commitment to the lowlanders. She did not have to travel far from the Citadel to find people to take her in. Still, she knew—as for the last time she looked back at the castle, its white walls gleaming in the moonlight—they would never accept her as one of them.

Many of the lowlanders sensed, rather than remembered, another era, an era long before this one when fair-skinned, straight-haired people like themselves had been dominant in the world. Then they had been the oppressors and those who now ruled from the Citadel with their dark skins and thick hair had been the oppressed. Now, deprived of the Citadel's power, Tamar knew that she would be shunned by some lowlanders and mistreated by others. Her resemblance to the Citadel's rulers could outweigh all her good works on the lowlanders' behalf. Well, even in the Citadel she had met distrust; not because of color, but because she was a woman, and because she challenged tradition by speaking out. It was her destiny, one she had made for herself. One she would continue to make on the unknown road ahead.

Shadowboxing:
Blacks, Jews and Games Scapegoats Play

Coalition building is an enterprise with valuable potential as long as its pursuit does not obscure the basic fact: nobody can free us but ourselves.

"Some black people will not be amused, Geneva, but I assume the Citadel tale's placing people of color in power is to illustrate that whites do not have a monopoly on the willingness to dominate a weaker group based on color."

"H'mm." She looked pensive, pained really, as though I had missed her meaning yet again. But she recovered, evidently on good behavior here on Afrolantica. "That's surely one message, but far more important is the unhappy truth that some subordinate group members will seek power at the expense of others less well off in their group."

"Or of another subordinate group," I offered. "I suspect that seeking advantage with more powerful whites is a factor in the division between the black and Jewish communities, despite the deep similarities of their historic oppression."

"Perhaps, friend, but neither side would admit to any such motivation. So, what we have is an unsettling and unsettled suspicion and below-the-surface hostility between both blacks and Jews."

"Hostility that must be a source of amusement to those far-right groups who would love to get rid of both blacks and Jews."

Geneva nodded in agreement. "Yes, and not just

81

the far right, friend. I sense that much of America views black/Jewish attacks and counter attacks interspersed by interminable meetings as a political sporting event. Two scapegoat groups going after each other for ten rounds and then making up until the next time.

"The boxing metaphor is off the mark. There are no official knockdowns here, but utilizing wealth and influence, Jews can and do cause a great deal of harm to individual blacks and black interests when they sense a conflict with their well-being. But for the most part, it's as if the scapegoats are shadow-boxing, each with an opponent that is not even in the ring."

Geneva smiled and nodded in agreement. Then she turned serious. "Of course, distrust and lack of respect will cause a great many Jews to stay on the sidelines in the Great Race Debate. If all the controversy turns out to worsen race relations, they won't want to suffer reprisals from angry whites. The fact that history teaches that when racial hostility increases in this country, anti-Semitic feeling increases as well will add to their concern, not alter their sit-it-out decision."

"True enough. There are Jews who will stand on the side of racial justice no matter the consequences. But others who claim to be friends insist all blacks condemn out-of-hand any black who they feel has done or said something disparaging about Jews. Usually, color is our only connection with the person who has upset them, but that doesn't seem to matter. It is a frustration to me and, I am sure, a great many black people."

"Calm down, friend. I thought you told me you were trying to understand these calls for condemnation, rather than simply castigate them."

"Actually, I've discussed the issue with a Jewish law teacher. He saw a parallel between the reaction of some Jews to the inflammatory statements made about them and my response to an incident that happened to me."

ᓚᡆᓚᡆᓚᡆ

I was working in my office at the law school on a late summer afternoon when someone knocked on my door. Thinking it a faculty member or someone from the administrative staff, I invited the person to come in. The door opened and I looked up to see a somewhat seedily dressed black man standing there.

"Are you the professor who publishes those stories with Geneva Crenshaw?"

"Yes," I said, thinking the fellow had purchased one of our books and wanted an autograph. I was wrong.

"My name's Nat T. I'm looking for Geneva Crenshaw. Where can I find her?" He remained standing at the door. Noting the anger in his voice, I got up and walked over to him.

"Mr. T, I take your question as a compliment, but I assure you that Geneva Crenshaw is a purely fictional character, a representation of many black women I have known and learned from during my life."

He would have none of it. "Man, don't put me off. I know she's real. And I also know she understands how this country works to keep us down."

"Are you a writer?"

He laughed. "No, man, but I can read. That woman is wasting her time trying to convince you of the obvious. When we get together, we are going to

83

organize black folks as never before. You wouldn't understand, so just give me Geneva Crenshaw's address or her phone number."

Nat T's intensity made me nervous. I wasn't sure whether he was mentally disturbed or just scarily purposeful.

"Look, Professor. Don't get me wrong. I'm not a nut. Fact is, ten years ago, I was a law student, going to a fancy law school just like this one. They flunked me out after my first year. The all-white faculty didn't like my black nationalist views.

"Well, I'm sorry," I said with a touch of unintended sarcasm, "but if you talked about a revolution instead of contracts and property, your teachers probably weren't impressed."

Nat T was not amused. "I was a good student," he retorted. "I worked hard. They decided I was too militant. I only wanted to understand how the law was able to preach justice and still keep my people down. I wanted maybe to teach others some day. They told me I would never make a good law teacher with my attitude. It's the story of my life. I have the brains, I work hard, but I lose jobs because I don't have the right 'attitude,' meaning I don't walk a racial tight rope trying to be myself and still not threaten white folks."

"Law schools grade exams anonymously to prevent bias of that character," I suggested. He just looked at me as though I was the most pathetically naive person he had ever met. I decided not to push the point.

"After they flunked me out and refused to give me another chance," he said, "my life kind of fell apart. I had always wanted to be a lawyer, a sort of legal Malcolm X. He was my hero. When I couldn't find a decent job with my undergraduate degree, my wife took our son and headed back to the West Coast where she had a job offer. On the way they were both killed in an auto crash."

"That's awful," I replied cautiously. "And you connect her tragic accident with your treatment by the law school?"

"Wouldn't you? That and the hostility of a society that brings us down and keeps us down. Professor, it's time we give back in kind the harm done to us because we are black."

"An eye for an eye," I responded, "is neither moral nor, for the most part, has it been how black people have responded to racist oppression."

"And look where we are as a result, or," and he looked hard at me, "where most of us are. Black people need to live by a rule of racial retaliation."

"Racial what?" I asked incredulously.

"Racial retaliation," he repeated. "In a society that has actively practiced racism since its inception, it's no surprise that except for some feeble, hard to enforce, anti-discrimination laws, whites can discriminate against blacks just for the hell of it. We don't respond in kind, and so they keep on doing it."

"Well," I conceded with some relief that he had switched his anger from me to the system. "I can hardly disagree with your assessment, but—"

"Professor, whites should know that their acts of discrimination have broad ramifications. They need to exercise due care in the light of this knowledge, and they should be held to full account for actions that are likely to set in motion devastating racial reactions."

"It's an interesting variation on standard court law, Mr. T, but not one the law and those who enforce it will take kindly to."

Nat T responded angrily. "You teach the law,

Professor, but you sure as hell don't understand it. The law is what the society wants it to be. Why do you think the law, including the U.S. Constitution, condoned slavery for all those years? Certainly not because it was right and moral. Slavery was profitable—the only morality this damn country cares about. When did slavery end? It ended when the big profits were going to factory owners exploiting white, wage slaves most of whom felt superior to blacks. We were left out. Well, no more. When white society sees blacks have stopped killing one another and turned their rage on the real causes of their desperation, whites will change and not one second before."

"With all your anger," I ventured, "you have a lot more faith than I do that this society will do other than strike back with a massive display of firepower."

Nat T ignored me and began describing in more detail than I really cared to hear how he was going to organize the black community and build an effective retaliatory force. He obviously had given the matter of revolution a great deal of thought.

He sensed what I was thinking. "You still think I'm crazy. But see, Professor, we've all been crazy to rely all these years on whites ever treating us decently unless they see something in it for them. Well, rather than moan about it, I'm going to show them that not treating us well is going to be very, very costly. They're putting all the young black men they can find in prison, and for as long as they can. But the brothers will get out someday with plenty of rage, no chance for a job, and no obligation to a society that has shut them out. I'm going to recruit them into a quiet force. No loud blustering about what we are going to do like the so-called militant black groups of the 1960s. We will simply do what is called for and fade back into the woodwork."

At that point, I had heard enough. I told Nat T that I really had to get back to work. He raised several more questions about Geneva Crenshaw: where did she work? When had I last seen her? When did I expect to see her again?

"I am sorry. She exists only in my imagination."

He shook his head. "Man, don't you understand? In denying Geneva Crenshaw's existence, you are denying your existence. There is no hope for you, man. No hope."

Nat T turned to leave and then turned back and faced me squarely.

"I'm going, but I'm telling you right now. I am coming back."

"Oh?" I remarked dubiously.

"Yes," he responded with that same seriousness. "Once I find Geneva Crenshaw and get our revolution started, one of my first missions will be to return and blow your head off."

I was unnerved, but I tried not to show it by questioning his priorities. "You know," I told him, "in order to reach my office, you will have to pass the offices of several of my white colleagues."

"I know that," he replied, "but the revolution must first deal with all you black tokens. As agents of the enemy, you are a danger. You do more damage with your token jobs than the real enemy."

"So," I said, feeling my anger rise, "your racial retaliation theory will begin at home?"

"It will begin with the enemy," he responded. Then, as suddenly and resolutely as he'd come, he left.

✧✧✧✧

I closed the door, returned to my desk, and tried to pull myself together. Feeling some ambivalence, I reached for the phone, my hand shaking, dialed the campus police and reported the incident. Then I heard my office door opening and, startled, looked up fearing it was Nat T again. Instead, it was Ben Hirsch, a member of the faculty, and visibly angry.

"Bell. Was that black guy, who just passed me in the hall, visiting you?"

I felt irritation replace my fears. "Believe it or not, Ben, not every black person in this building is here to visit me even though, despite my best efforts, I remain one of only three persons of color on this faculty."

Ignoring my criticism, Ben blurted out. "I asked him where he was going and he called me a white S.O.B. Said it was none of my damn business. Pushed me aside and walked out of the building. I called campus police. I keep telling the dean we need better security around this place. As it is, anybody can walk in here."

"Meaning, Ben, any black can walk in here and get upset when you question him about his business, a process I would guess you don't do with any of the dozens of whites who walk through here all the time. Am I right?"

"O.K., I get your point, but still it's upsetting—accosted in your own building."

"The building is open to the public." Angry as well as shaken, I sat down wearily at my desk. Hirsch, slim, intense, rather nerdy looking, just stood there until I waved him to a chair. He was far from the person I wanted to be with at that moment. We seldom talk. He's a staunch supporter of Israel where he travels frequently and consults with the government. He seems to be involved in every Jewish cause. And since he visited the death camps in Poland, Majdonek, Treblinka, and Auschwitz, his commitment to Judaism has become a personal crusade, one I gather that annoys others on the heavily Jewish faculty who are embarrassed by Hirsch's super-Jewish posturing.

Hirsch dismisses their criticism and publicly calls them assimilationists unwilling to identify with issues vital to the survival of the Jewish community here and in Israel. As a result of those quotes—the media loved them—few Jewish faculty members have much to do with him. So much for my father's dinner table lectures that blacks, if we were ever to get ahead, had to learn to stick together like the Jews.

To break the uneasy silence, I told him of Nat's visit.

"Oh," he replied. "That's serious. Did you call the police?" I nodded.

"A bad scene, Bell. Now you know why I and other Jews get so upset and respond so heatedly when Louis Farrakhan and other black nationalists attack us."

"Somehow, Ben, I don't see the connection between my run-in with Nat T and the full-throttle rage of virtually every Jewish group and most individual Jews when one black leader makes comments they deem anti-Semitic."

"Well, look at you. Still shaken. And why not? A threat like you received, filled with so much venom. It's very distressing. You don't like threats. Jews don't like threats."

"Wait just a damn minute, Ben. To my knowledge, Minister Farrakhan has never threatened to kill any Jews."

Undeterred by my rising anger, Ben pressed his

point. "Not directly. Both his threats and Nat T's are for the future, but you surely cannot deny that your automatic response to Nat T's future threat was immediate defense and then counter attack. You called the police. Right?"

"O.K., I did and felt some guilt for hoping they would get him and put him away."

"But you didn't feel sufficient sympathy for the cruel hand that fate had dealt him to simply ignore his threat on your life."

"Not at that moment, I didn't. I admit it, but it was crazy. I mean what charges could I bring? A threat to kill me at some time in the future? Likely, Nat T's threat was an assault, but in the context of crime in today's world, who would take it seriously? I would have come to my senses at some point which is more than a lot of Jews seem able to do in the face, not of threats, but of simply verbal criticism and abuse by Minister Louis Farrakhan, and his now-deposed spokesperson, Khalid Muhammad."

"Well, Nat T's threats, and Farrakhan's, while only those of individuals, remind us of group hostility in the society aimed at you as a successful black and me as a Jew."

"Ben, not only don't I see a connection between my reaction to Nat T's threat and the overreaction of Jews whenever a black says something negative about your group, I really resent your effort to compare the two situations."

"That's because you don't want to see it. Look, the Jewish reaction is quite similar to yours against Nat T. Jews are saying, 'After all we have been through, why should we have to be subjected to gratuitous insults by demagogues seeking to use hate tactics to gain power at our expense?' We know the tactic and have been victimized by it over the centuries. But no more. The place to draw the 'never again' line is right here."

"Ben, give me a break. The Jewish response to what they consider anti-Semitic attacks makes my call for police action seem mild in comparison—but no less futile. The Nation of Islam has been castigated in full-page ads and dozens of opinion columns. The U.S. Senate has voted on a resolution condemning Muhammed's speeches. And to what end? Like Brer Rabbit after being tossed in the briar patch by Brer Fox, the Nation of Islam spokespersons are glorying in levels of public attention and acclaim from their followers that they could not have purchased with love or money.

"And don't get me started, Ben. Charging he was anti-Semitic, some Jewish groups supported a major, though unsuccessful, effort to remove Professor Leonard Jeffries from his teaching post at CUNY. The matter wound up in the courts.[1] And according to Wellesley College Professor Tony Martin, college administrators and Jewish groups have tried to have him removed as a result of his use of a book deemed disparaging of Jews.[2] He has a book, detailing these efforts."[3]

"There are more such instances, but you get the point."

"Which is?"

"Which is that you simply can't compare my call to the police after Nat T's threat with these all-out campaigns to use position and influence to punish black academics; efforts, I might add, that encourage rather than discourage the verbal attacks I assume Jews are trying to stop."

"O.K., Bell, that point may be something of a stretch, but let me try another tack. I think Nat T's threat was particularly upsetting because at some level it reminded you of the broad range of hostility in the society aimed at blacks, and particularly at successful blacks by some black militants. Your reaction to Nat T was not only to what he said but also to what he symbolized. He served as a reminder that he is neither alone nor entirely inaccurate in viewing successful blacks as the enemy—no matter how hard someone like you works for the progress of all blacks. Am I right?"

"No, Ben. Success for blacks means you are treated with suspicion by some blacks and become a threat to some whites. It's the price of 'moving on up.' Given the growing gap in income opportunity among blacks, it's a wonder that there aren't more blacks like Nat T who believe that blacks with some status have gained it at their expense and are thus their enemy. As economic conditions worsen for poorer blacks, the numbers of those who share Nat T's opinion will increase. I am sorry, Ben, I don't see any comparison between the Catch-22 plight of successful blacks and that of Jews."

"I didn't say the situations are exactly the same."

"Because you can't."

"Listen. You speak of the isolation of successful blacks—and the sense of unease based on that isolation—based on your experience."

"I do, and you want me to believe that Jews share my sense of isolation?"

"You don't have to listen to me. As Paul Berman writes: 'The styles of Jewish New World success follow patterns that were established in the Old World ghettos, and the successes themselves are fated now and then to call up, out of the creepier depths of Christian civilization, the old paranoid accusations about conspiracies and evil.'⁴

"You see, Berman is saying that our outsider status is not altered merely by Jews fleeing from the Old World to the New. He writes: 'Even the fat-and-happiest of American Jews has to shudder at the spectacle, which is always taking place, of some eminent person, not only spokesmen of the Nation of Islam, standing up to give the ancient libels a fresh new airing.'"[5]

"I understand the symbolic fear, Ben, but Jews are white, and many are successful, despite being Jews."

"True enough, Bell, but success can increase rather than diminish a sense of fear. For many Jews, Louis Farrakhan and the Nation of Islam evoke these fears. Unlike blacks, it is true that most Jews are successful in all the ways this society measures success. And, yet there is justifiable concern that their very success has heightened rather than reduced the hostility vented against them—simply because they are Jews."

"But why Farrakhan and a few, little-known black scholars, when neo-Nazi groups are openly threatening Jews and doing so while wearing Nazi uniforms?"

"We oppose all anti-Semitism, but Farrakhan gets far more publicity for his statements than do most of those far-right nuts."

"Sure he does in substantial part because Jews react with such vehemence. It gives the media a field day and many Americans a chance to criticize blacks without seeming racist."

"Reactions to fear are not always rational. You saw that yourself just an hour ago. I agree with writer-activist Letty Cottin Pogrebin who fears 'the dominant majority may suddenly turn against the Jews (as some Americans did during the energy crisis and the Gulf War), fear of possible peril to the state of Israel (every Jew's haven of last resort), and fear of the slippery slope that propelled another "civilized society" from spewing hate to building gas chambers."[6]

"She surely can't be comparing the current suffering of blacks with Jews' fear of potential suffering."

"No, but she explains 'for Jews one generation removed from the Holocaust, the fear is real and the vulnerability deeply felt.'"[7]

"Ben, I will take your 'fear of the future based on the past' point on faith. But it doesn't explain the vehemence of Jewish attacks on blacks who have upset them."

"It's a form of aggressive denial. Jews hope that by soundly squashing the relatively powerless individual whose words upset you, you are symbolically defusing the major powers in the society whom you fear to upset and refuse to challenge."

"That's not it at all. Face it, Ben, Jews jump on a relatively powerless black man who taunts them as a warning to those forces who, while less vocal, are far more capable of doing Jews in—when the time is right."

"Bell, your castigation is causing you to miss the similarity of your response."

"I called the police, Ben. I didn't run around trying to get other down-and-out blacks to denounce Nat T for threatening me. That would be stupid. And it is equally stupid when Jews demand that I denounce something Farrakhan has said. Stupid and, I will say it, racist."

"There is that overused word again."

"Overused? Hardly. Look, Ben, do any of those Jews who demand that black spokespersons drop everything and denounce the rantings of a few blacks have any sense of what is happening to black people in this society?"

"You're surely not going to blame the plight of blacks on Jews?"

"No, though those neoconservative, Jewish scholars who have bad-mouthed affirmative action to death are certainly responsible for some of the distress. As, I might add, are a great many Jews who don't agree with the attacks but don't challenge them, thereby providing a silent acquiescence.

"Oh, I understand the determination when Jews say 'Never again.' Fair enough, but while they are demanding a public rebuttal to every anti-Jewish statement some black makes, blacks are being eliminated by a more subtle but no less deadly holocaust.

Ben started to protest. I wouldn't stop to hear it. "I know. Many Jews feel they have an exclusive right to that word. But listen. If the nation's policies toward blacks were revised to require weekly, random round-ups of several hundred blacks who were then taken to a secluded place and shot, that policy would be more dramatic, but hardly different in result than the policies now in effect, and about which most of us feel powerless to change. Nat T knows this, and he views me as a danger precisely because he believes I don't see or, rather, don't want to acknowledge this quiet holocaust."

Ben started for the door, shaking his head. "I understand your position and I think you understand mine. At some rather basic level of abstraction we will have to agree to disagree."

"Fine with me, Ben. I just wish more Jews would keep in mind what Professor Delores Aldridge said, namely that 'both Jews and blacks occupy a somewhat precarious position in American society and culture. Neither group has the power to determine the destiny of the other. They both warily monitor the mood of the White American mainstream.' Then she adds: 'Allies do not have to be good friends.' In my view, that means a basic respect, including a willingness to view the entirety of an ally's performance, not judge and condemn based on a few sound bites."

Ben's response was interrupted by my phone ringing. It was the campus police. I listened, promised to call back in a few minutes, and hung up.

"Well, Ben. The police have picked up Nat T. They want me to come down and press charges."

"And after criticizing Jews for overresponding to anti-Semitic comments, you're not going to do it, right?"

It was hard to miss the sarcasm in his question. "I keep telling you, Ben, the situations are not anomalous. Because I am making the charge and Nat T with his revolutionary outlook is the kind of black man this society wants to put away, they will prosecute and likely convict him. That will provide me and others with a semblance of safety, but no more than that."

"So, what are you going to do?"

"Suppose Nat T was a very angry member of the Nation of Islam and had come to your office door, repeated every charge against Jews that some members of the group have made and then threatened to kill you at some future date. Would you press charges?"

"In a heart beat. And I would do it with special glee if it was Minister Farrakhan himself, an obvious charlatan for whom you seem to be a self-appointed apologist. Good luck with your decision. I have to go." Ben opened the door, prepared to leave.

"Oh no you don't. The sooner Jews learn that Minister Farrakhan is not your worst nightmare, the better off you will be. Come back here and sit your butt down. Now listen. Like him or not, Minister Farrakhan has a large following in the black community. He draws tremendous crowds. And in his three-hour speeches, he does more than castigate white people. He also criticizes some black leaders, ministers and gays. But, his basic sermon, beyond his provocative verbiage and stinging condemnations, is a quite conservative message of self-help."

"Jews obviously don't agree with you, nor, I might add, do a lot of black people, including Judge A. Leon Higginbotham and Julian Bond. They both boycotted the 'Million Man March,' because Farrakhan organized it. But not you." Quickly scanning my book shelves, he pulled a volume down and waved it at me. "When Farrakhan put out his book a few years ago, *A Torchlight for America*,[8] you actually wrote a blurb for the jacket." He read it: "Unlike those conservatives, black and white, who only preach self-help to the poor as a crowd-pleasing abstraction, Farrakhan's formulas emphasize the Nation of Islam's experience in educating black children, rehabilitating black prisoners, ridding black communities of drug dealers, and rebuilding respect for self—the essential prerequisite for individuals determined to maintain the struggle against the racism that burdens our lives and, unless curbed, will destroy this country.'"[9] He tossed the book on my desk with a dramatic flourish.

"Ben, have you read the book?" He shook his head defiantly.

"You and a lot of others should read the book. Or, at least read his speeches.[10] Then you can criticize the work and not the selected excerpts that the media plays over and over." I picked up the book and put it back on the bookshelf. "I certainly don't expect many Jews to agree with my assessment. But their disagreement takes the form of retaliation. Entities deemed supportive of the Nation of Islam or its spokespersons have been threatened with economic reprisals, and black leaders and groups—though they have no more in common than color with the Nation of Islam's speakers—have been urged to condemn the speakers. Those who refuse are interpreted as supporting the attackers."

"I am not going to defend every statement Jews make anymore than I expect you to condemn every statement that Farrakhan makes. But you seem all too ready to defend whatever he does or says."

"I really don't, Ben. But I am moved to his side by the 'take no prisoners' attitude of his attackers; for example, when Benjamin F. Chavis, the former NAACP executive director, warned his Anti-Defamation League (A.D.L.) counterpart, Abraham Foxman, that continued A.D.L. attacks on Farrakhan could create precisely what Jewish leaders say they fear: black anti-Semitism. Foxman acknowledged the risk, but said he was willing to take it, warning on his part that if African American leaders do not clearly distance themselves from views such as Farrakhan's, 'it will undermine the moral underpinnings of a coalition.'[11]

"You know, Ben, this pattern of hard-line response to blacks and civil rights policies deemed threatening to Jews didn't begin with Louis Farrakhan. In fact, some of what you see as my defense of Farrakhan is my reaction to how some Jewish groups have treated other black leaders."

"For example?"

"Let's start with former U. N. Ambassador Andrew Young, who met secretly with the Palestinians. Young, a black man with impeccable credentials who had earned the respect of virtually all blacks, was hounded out of his job."

"Most of us plead a special sensitivity when issues of Israel's survival are on the table."

"That's just it. Andrew Young was working to protect Israel in the only way it can be protected—at the negotiating table with the Palestinians. That's obvious to everyone now. Young had the vision early on.

"But Ben, the Jesse Jackson case is the classic example of the retaliatory response. Jackson has done everything but offer to jump off a tall building to explain his position on Israel and Palestine and to atone for his 'hymietown' remark, seemingly, to no avail. Despite his leadership role, many Jewish groups will not forgive him. As one Jewish friend who opposes such tactics put it, they are 'demanding penance without hope of forgiveness.'"

"Are you telling me, Bell, that Jews shouldn't respond vigorously to statements they deem anti-Semitic?"

"Far from it, Ben, but it seems to me an example of 'piling on' when Jewish groups ignore the total record of blacks like Jackson and use their greater influence in the community to block political aspirations and other activity not connected with the statements or actions that offended them. In addition, there is the use of economic clout to threaten business enterprises of those deemed dangerous to Jewish interests. Thus, Jewish groups led by the Anti-Defamation League have used their influence to prevent security firms organized by the Nation of Islam from obtaining or holding contracts with public housing authorities to provide the projects with much-needed security. The fact that these companies have a record of bringing peace and order to public housing when police have failed was of no concern to A.D.L. Their single aim was to get rid of groups they deemed anti-Semitic. And Ben, in my view, their actions are despicable."

"I heard that the Nation of Islam has not always been successful in reducing crime in their security businesses and that they had financial problems."

"That's not the point, Ben, and surely not why the A.D.L. and other Jewish groups intervened. They wanted to retaliate without any concern that the Nation of Islam companies were providing jobs and building entrepreneurial skills in communities much in need of both.[12]

"I didn't say Jews can't be excessive—like any other group trying to protect their interests."

"But why so much militancy at our expense? Ben, I wish the Nation of Islam security contract case, and the clobbering of Andy Young and Jesse Jackson were exceptional cases. They are not. The pressures against blacks who upset Jews adhere to a pattern.

"Writer-educator Haki R. Madhubuti recalls years ago mounting a protest against John Johnson, the publisher of *Ebony, Jet*, and other black publications.[13] The protest followed Johnson's discontinuance of *Black World*, a progressive political journal and the dismissal of the magazine's editor, Hoyt Fuller, a highly respected journalist. Madhubuti reports that a large group set up picket lines around Johnson's new, multistory building on Michigan Avenue in downtown Chicago. Within the first hour of the demonstration, Mr. Johnson himself appeared, and invited the group inside for a talk. There, Johnson told the group that he had halted the publication of *Black World* and fired Fuller for refusing to cease publishing the Palestinian side of the Middle East struggle and the African support for that struggle. He did so, he said, 'because Jewish businessmen threatened to pull their advertising out of *Ebony* and *Jet* magazines and would have convinced their white friends to do the same if the Middle East coverage didn't stop.'[14]

"Madhubuti and the other protesters, learning of this exercise of overwhelming power, said: 'We were stunned into a weakening silence. Our responses were few because we knew it was both an economic and political decision and as an astute businessman, Mr. Johnson did what he felt was best for his company'".[15]

Ben sat quietly for a time, deep in thought. "Let me ask you this. How do the Jewish boycotts or their threat you complain about, how do they differ from those blacks have used since the 1930s to get jobs in white-owned and—more recently—Korean-owned businesses located in black communities?"

"It may not be one you'll accept, Ben, but there is a clear distinction based on the relative power of the two groups. Blacks resorted to boycotts as a substitute for political and economic power in an effort to pressure businesses to treat blacks fairly. Jewish groups utilize their formidable economic power to intimidate blacks into halting actions that Jews find offensive."

"Why can't you acknowledge the determination of Jews to do what they felt was necessary to protect Israel and to strike hard at the first instance of hate that, unchecked, can lead to mass murder?"

"I can't accept running rough shod over a black publisher because his small, intellectual magazine is appropriately critical of how Israel has treated the Palestinians. It should not be a surprise that many blacks resent the use of Jewish political and economic power in this way."

Ben seemed taken aback. I was standing and rather loudly proclaiming my views.

"Jews will align with conservatives who care little about them, but who adopt a pro-Israel stance as a means of muting criticism of them on other issues."

"I don't hear you getting that upset over the KKK, Bell. Why is it only Jews that upset you so?"

"It's not only Jews, but it also has to do with power. The KKK is relatively powerless. And that is just the damn problem, Ben. Many blacks, not just me, get very upset over the willingness of American Jews to protect Israel—regardless of what it does, including killing protesters, doing business with the old South Africa, the list goes on. We have been much too reticent about expressing publicly our resentment at pressure tactics of this type."

I thought about it a moment as I tried to calm down. How do I explain my silence and the silence of so many other blacks? Was it to keep from stepping on the toes of our Jewish friends? Was it a rational decision that we have more important priorities demanding our energies? Or, to be honest, were we quiet because, as Adolph Reed put it, we feared Jewish economic clout, the same fear that Madhubuti's group experienced?

Analyzing the failure of most black leaders to criticize Israel's relationship with South Africa, Adolph Reed did not claim blacks are duped, co-opted, or coerced to pursue 'Jewish interests.' Rather:

> The environmental condition of greater Jewish institutional entrenchment combines with interracialism to structure a context of action in which rational, independent articulation and pursuit of pragmatic goals

by black elites requires a nonreciprocal attentiveness to Jewish organizational interests. . . . Jewish Zionism, to put the matter somewhat provocatively, overrides Black Zionism—even in the black organizational apparatus![16]

Probably reading my silence as seething, Ben tried a more conciliatory approach. "I am not sure," he said quietly, "that the more sensitive portions of the Jewish community understands how strongly you feel about some of these issues."

"How could they if we don't sound off to them the way I've been sounding off to you. Blacks should be no less willing to speak out than Michael Lerner did in condemning 'some in the Jewish world who for decades have used the Holocaust and the history of our very real oppression as an excuse to deny our own racism toward blacks or Palestinians.' In the frantic effort to make it in America, Lerner writes, 'we also began to buy the racist assumptions of this society and to forget our own history of oppression.'"

"Lerner might have a point" Ben said. "Maybe because blacks have been quiet about actions of Jews they did not agree with, they expected Jews to be tolerant about anti-Semitic statements. But whatever our misjudgments, shouldn't we stand shoulder to shoulder in opposing hateful statements, whether hurled against blacks or Jews?"

"That question, as New York State Senator David A. Paterson explained, must be answered in the light of the tolerance of pervasive racism tolerated against blacks. With such figures as Jesse Helms in the Senate and Rush Limbaugh as a national icon, blacks are very suspicious of white efforts to focus our antiracist efforts on any black political leader—

including the appalling statements of Khalid Muhammad.[17]

"Paterson acknowledges the historical reluctance of blacks to engage in public criticism, adding 'for generations, whites have called on black leaders to denounce other blacks' offensive or radical ideas. Many leaders have actually been denounced as a result of such pleas, leading to crippling battles among black political leaders. Betrayals and self-defeating efforts to exclude rival leaders have undermined hard-fought efforts to gain and hold political power all across the country."[18]

"I didn't say it wouldn't take political courage to speak out against a popular leader."

"But courage in whose cause, Ben. Blacks complain, with some justified bitterness, that spokespersons of other ethnic groups are not asked to stand and condemn anti-Semitic statements made by individuals within those groups. Thus, Senator Edward Kennedy is not pressured to condemn the clearly anti-Semitic rantings of say Pat Buchanan, because they are both Irish. No one insists that John Kenneth Galbraith denounce the anti-Semitism of David Duke simply because both men are of Scotch ancestry."

"That would be ridiculous," Ben blurted out. "They have nothing in common." He seemed to realize what he was saying and his voice trailed off.

I tried but could not resist. "I rest my case, Ben. I don't know whether or not it's a conscious action, but those demands show that, Jews, like most whites, view blacks as society's 'other.' It's a role of social subordination that Jews have had to play as much as any other people in history. In the status of 'other,' there is no distinction among the group. The unsettling statements of one can be 'canceled' by the denunciation of another."

"Letty Cottin Pogrebin would disagree with you, Bell. She says that 'the need to hear reassuring words from blacks can be read as a measure of the high regard Jews have for the opinion of the African American community', and that 'the demand for a response from black voices bespeaks a greater recognition and respect than the rest of America extends to the authority and power of black leadership.'"[19]

"Letty, I am certain, speaks sincerely for herself and, likely, many other Jews. The chapter on black-Jewish relations in her book, *Deborah, Golda, and Me*, is one of the most objective and thorough I have read on this subject.[20] But Ben, blacks have been down so long that they recognize demands based on dominance when they hear them—even those made in good faith."

"Oh, come on, Bell. The words dominance and good faith seem contradictions. People like Letty Pogrebin are either speaking in good faith or they aren't."

"Standing alone, maybe, Ben, but consider the context. First, the demands are unilateral. That is, blacks must condemn statements deemed by Jews to be anti-Semitic, but there is no similar willingness of those Jews to condemn publicly any racist statements and actions by Jews."

"Meaning what?"

"Meaning, why should Michael Lerner be among the few Jews ready to speak out publicly about the hypocrisy among 'Jewish neoconservatives at *Commentary* magazine and Jewish neoliberals at the *New Republic* [who] have led the assault on affirmative action (despite the fact that one of its greatest beneficiaries has been Jewish women); have blamed the persistence of racism on the victims' culture of poverty; and have delighted in the prospect of throwing black women and children off welfare as soon as possible.'[21]

"In addition, the demands are limited to blacks. Where is the pressure that Jewish groups should be placing on right-wing groups and their leaders who are ready to match anti-Semitic words with deeds? Micah Sifry, noting that the Anti-Defamation League comes down far harder on blacks making anti-Semitic statements than those whites in high positions, writes: 'There is no question the A.D.L. takes its minority anti-Semitism seriously, as well it should. But what about anti-Semitism elsewhere, among the white majority and by the powerful?' Sifry makes the point that as some Jewish groups have turned more conservative, they tend to excuse the anti-Semitism of those on the right while bearing down on blacks.[22]

"Sifry's long article offers impressive support for his position, but it is not one likely to influence A.D.L. leaders who sat out the David Duke races in 1990 and 1991 for senator and governor, allegedly because of its tax-exempt status, but quietly circulated a nineteen-page memo to reporters detailing Jesse Jackson's past statements regarding Jews, even before the 'Hymietown' furor broke.[23] When the 'Hymietown' furor broke, Sifry reports: 'A.D.L. officials leapt at the opportunity to nail him as an anti-Semite. Apologies were of no use. "He could light candles every Friday night, and grow side curls, and it still wouldn't matter . . . he's a whore," Nathan Perlmutter, then the A.D.L.'s director, told CBS News reporter Bob Faw.'"[24]

"There you go again, Bell. I told you before I'm not going to defend every stupid thing Jews say and do. And moreover—" Ben said, his voice rising. He was interrupted by my telephone.

"Saved by the bell," I thought. It was the police offering to give me a ride to the station. I told them to meet me outside in ten minutes.

"So, you are going to press charges?"

"I'm going over to review the situation with the police, maybe get a chance to talk to Nat T."

"Not going to play King Solomon are you? Remember, he was one of us."

"No, but I want you to consider the relevance to my situation of Andrew Young's comment about Jews: 'Jews' quite understandable determination expressed in the phrase, "never again," is not inconsistent with a willingness to forgive.'"

"I don't see any relevance."

"That's because you don't have to see it. And for the reasons you don't, the tension and distrust between blacks and Jews that goes all the way back, is not likely to end. We are far apart economically but closer in status than a lot of Jews and blacks want to think about. So both groups are extra sensitive about everything."

"Well," Ben observed, "our discussion this afternoon proves that."

I nodded. "But it's not hopeless. I am confident that my relationship with Jews who I know and trust will continue. They will agree with much of what I say about race and, from time to time, we will join in projects that serve our interests. No doubt, other groups of blacks and Jews will do the same. That may be as close to an alliance as any of us can get, and it may be enough to frustrate those in power who must enjoy the battling between the two groups most likely to be sacrificed 'in the nation's interest' if the need arises."

Ben extended his hand. "I really have to go. I hope it works out at the police station." He closed the door quietly as he left.

Gathering my papers, I came across a quote and made a mental note to send it to Ben. In an effort to avoid the fate of all societal scapegoats, Albert Vorspan and David Saperstein, two leaders of the Reform movement, wrote in their book, *Tough Choices: Jewish Perspectives on Social Justice:*

> We can find no safety in turning inward upon ourselves, severing our links with the general community. We can find safety only if we help America deal not only with the symptoms—hatred, rage, bigotry—but with the root problems of our society—slums, powerlessness, decay of our cities, and unemployment, which spawn the evils of bigotry and conflict. Our task as Jews must go beyond the defensive job of countering the attacks of anti-Semitism to helping bring about a just and peaceful society.[25]

Why, I wondered, can't statements like that get the public attention the neoconservative Jews are able to command with their latest blast against affirmative action and welfare mothers? Heading for the door, I knew the answer. It was more than a question. It was the problem.

Paul Robeson:
Doing the State Some Service

An individual whose actions against racism threaten the powerful must be prepared endure both the condemnation of enemies and the abandonment by friends.

"If my informal debate with Ben Hirsch is an example of what we can expect from the Great Race Debate, Geneva, then I don't think we will get much support."

"Don't be so pessimistic. If all whites had been as willing to debate their whiteness as Jews have their differences with blacks—"

"My point, exactly. I am not sure all those black-Jewish discussion groups make much of a difference."

"Some do. Some don't. Your discussion with Professor Hirsch should have made clear that coalitions with other groups should be sought but not relied on."

"Maybe. But the fragility of those alliances indicates how important it is that we recognize those among us with legitimate leadership qualities."

"Easier stated than accomplished, friend. America recognizes, rewards, and anoints as leaders those blacks—most of whom have no following—with whom it feels comfortable. It disparages and far worse those it deems uncontrollable or dangerous; even when they speak for most of us.

"The record is sobering, Geneva. W.E.B. Du Bois, our foremost intellectual, and Marcus Garvey, a leader of millions, were exiled. David Walker, a courageous, pre-Civil War writer, simply disappeared. Martin Luther King, Malcolm X, Medgar Evers, Fred Hampton and Lord knows how many lesser-known blacks were murdered. Then, there is the special case of Paul Robeson who became famous, not as a political leader, but as one of the great actors and singers of his time."

"It's a sad commentary, friend, but many young people have never heard of Robeson."

"Sad, Geneva, and as true for some not so young who know all about the current rap stars, Hollywood heroes, and sports figures. It's too bad, for as the son of a former slave, Paul Robeson was a true role model. His story deserves to serve as an illustration of one of the legacies. Perhaps in these times, the most important of them."

"The basic facts of his life are readily available," Geneva said. "Robeson was born in 1898, he rose from humble beginnings to become one of the most distinguished Americans of the twentieth century. No mere celebrity, Robeson was a modern-day Renaissance man. After graduating with Phi Beta Kappa honors from Rutgers University, where he twice received All-America football awards, he attended Columbia Law School and practiced briefly at a large law firm before becoming discouraged by the racism he encountered there.

"He turned to the theater and, performing in Eugene O'Neill's plays during the early 1920s, established himself as a brilliant actor. His tremendous bass-baritone voice gave him access to concert stages, and for two decades he was hailed as one of the greatest bass-baritones in the world. In the course of his many travels abroad, he was lionized. He played the title role in the 1943 Broadway pro-

duction of *Othello*, which ran a record 296 perfor-
mances. His acting in that play earned him, in 1944,
the Academy of Arts and Letters' Gold Medal for best
diction in the American theater and the Donaldson
Award for best actor.

"Robeson championed the cause of the
oppressed throughout his life, insisting that as an
artist he had no choice but to do so. A trip to the
Soviet Union early in his career had made him a life-
long friend of the USSR, which in 1952 awarded him
the Stalin Peace Prize. Following World War II, when
he took an uncompromising stand against segregation and lynching in the United States and advocated
friendship with the Soviet Union, a long, intense campaign was mounted against him. Thereafter he was
unable to earn a living as an artist in the United
States and was also denied a passport. Finally in
1958 he was allowed to go to Great Britain. He
returned in 1963 in ill health and spent the last years
of his life in seclusion. He died at age 78 in 1976.[1] In
my view, he was one of our greatest heroes."

I nodded my agreement. "I don't have a story as
such, but I want to offer a testament to Robeson that
will provide a meaningful message in the Great Race
Debate."

cisoclacio

Paul Robeson's life, like great art, is treasured
as much for the images it evokes as for the
story it portrays. At one level, one can view the obvious parallel of Robeson's contributions with those of
other well-known blacks who paid a large price for
their outspoken challenges to racial injustice. At
another level, with Robeson's life as model, the significant but less well-known sacrifice of other blacks
can be more easily recognized and appreciated.

Consider Tommie Smith and John Carlos. In accepting their gold and bronze medals in the 1968 Olympics, these black athletes mounted the victory podium and, as the national anthem played, bowed their heads, each man thrust high a black gloved fist in protest against racial strife in America. Their protest was memorable, coming as it did at the height of the Black Power Movement. It became a defining symbol—along with the urban rebellions—of black peoples' unwillingness to accept patiently the discrimination which the Supreme Court had outlawed a dozen years before.

While virtually all black people cheered the protest, most whites were appalled. They likely applauded when the U.S. Olympic Committee indignantly dismissed Smith and Carlos from the team. Both men suffered through years of job discrimination by employers and boycotts by sports promoters. It was the usual penalty paid by blacks who failed to combine their success with that deference signaling their understanding that triumph on the field has not altered their subordinate status in life.

Significantly, the retaliatory actions against Smith and Carlos have not dimmed the memory of that event. Back in the early 1970s, I was about to publish the first law school text devoted to issues of race and racism. As both epigraph and notice that the book would treat discrimination as the evil it is rather than a subject that would be examined "neutrally," I included a photograph of the Smith-Carlos protest and dedicated the book to all those who throughout this country's history have risked its wrath to protest its faults. I called the black athletes' protest:

The dramatic finale of an
Extraordinary achievement
Performed for a nation which
Had there been a choice
Would have chosen others, and
If given a chance
Will accept the achievement
And neglect the achievers.
Here, with simple gesture, they
Symbolize a people whose patience
With exploitation will expire with
The dignity and certainty
With which it has been endured . . .
Too long.[2]

The Olympic achievements of Carlos and Smith and the meaning of the nation's reaction to their protest are made clear by comparing it with Paul Robeson's experience. The lesson is clear. No degree of success or superiority in athletics, art, or scholarship insulates black criticism of white racism against swift and certain retaliation. Indeed, the higher the public platform provided by the society's recognition of that success, the more certain that whites will react to criticism, even though undeniably true, as an unforgivable betrayal. Robeson's experience then provides a prophetic paradigm for us all. And yet, Robeson's outspoken stance against American racism, even his too trusting attraction to communism and Russia, served well both the nation and its black citizens.

During World War II, as in earlier conflicts, blacks were at first excluded or segregated. The racial pattern was set at the start of the Revolutionary War when the Continental Congress proclaimed that it would not recruit Indians, vagabonds, or Negroes. When the enemy's challenge became threatening and the number of whites willing to serve proved less than the need, blacks were called upon and responded without rancor or regret. At war's end, the achievements were accepted and the achievers neglected; except that "neglect" inaccurately describes the reign of lynching and terror that was the black man's portion after each of the wars, including World Wars I and II.

World War II had devastated Western colonial powers. Nonwhite peoples were demanding an end to capitalist occupation and exploitation by Western nations. Communism offered a powerful alternative that both challenged and evoked great fear in this country. Paul Robeson, an international figure, by giving voice both here and abroad to what every black person knew about racism and capitalist exploitation, invested that knowledge with a legitimacy that is the prerequisite for serious opposition.

And, as if that were not enough, Robeson preached the doctrine unholy to guardians of the status quo that the working classes, black and white, were not only brothers, but suffered the same exploitation, a truth quite intentionally (and all too easily) hidden from lower-class whites by appeals to racism propounded by upper-class whites from the earliest days of American history to the present. Any assumption that Robeson's right of free speech encompassed such inflammatory truths proved naive in the extreme. When he proclaimed, as he did in his autobiography, *Here I Stand*, that the enemies are the "white folks on top," and dared suggest that American blacks might not so compliantly fight for America in some future war against a non racist country,[3] the retaliation that followed was as fierce as it was inevitable.

That policy-makers in this country recognized and determined to eliminate this formidable black danger to the economic status quo is evidenced by the systematic and blatant violation of Robeson's constitutional rights, admittedly accomplished to shut him up. When Robeson in 1950 demanded to know why his passport had been canceled, State Department officials said it was because he refused to sign the non-Communist affiliation oath, but they promised to return it if Robeson would sign a statement promising not to make any speeches when he was abroad.[4] He refused.

Robeson was barred from leaving the country, and was denied access to concert halls and lecture platforms at home. But his message had been heard. And if far fewer rank and file Americans heeded his advice than he had hoped, far more policy-makers than have ever acknowledged it learned from Robeson that to preserve the Union and their preeminent positions in it, a Twentieth Century equivalent of the Emancipation Proclamation would be necessary.

In an effort to limit the effect of Robeson's speeches condemning American racism, policy-makers and the media recruited well-known blacks to refute them. In an excess of patriotism over experience, some blacks did so. Among them was the baseball hero, Jackie Robinson, who had benefitted from Robeson's work against discrimination in professional baseball. He testified against Robeson before the House Committee on Un-American Activities. The baseball player's prepared statement was carefully worded only to condemn as "silly" Robeson's assertion that blacks would not fight for this country. He defended Robeson's right to his personal views and acknowledged the real injustices blacks suffer.

Robeson's enemies really didn't care what Jackie Robinson said. His appearance was comment enough—especially to the press, which eagerly reported the negative in Robinson's remarks, while ignoring the more positive balance.[5] In their turn, the leaders of the major civil rights organizations deemed it important to prove their own loyalties by condemning Robeson. Walter White, Executive Director of the NAACP, in a devastatingly critical article in *Ebony* magazine, described Robeson as a "bewildered man who is more to be pitied than damned."[6]

Paul Robeson, while a lawyer, deeply committed to civil rights, never had his name on any of the legal briefs in the school desegregation litigation that led in 1954 to the Supreme Court's decision in *Brown v. Board of Education.* Indeed, as those cases slowly made their way through the courts in the early 1950s, the government's campaign against Robeson had succeeded in portraying him as an enemy of his people and a pawn of Communist Russia. And yet, it is clear today that his strong condemnations of American racism out of court were as effective as any of the arguments propounded by lawyers who have received due credit for their roles in that landmark litigation. Robeson had stated the unstatable. By urging blacks not to reject communism until the free world proved it has a better deal,[7] he enabled NAACP legal brief-writers to warn the Supreme Court that the "Survival of our country in the present international situation is inevitably tied to resolution of this domestic issue."[8]

Consider also the U.S. Government's Amicus Curiae brief before the Supreme Court in *Brown*:

It is in the context of the present world struggle between freedom and tyranny that the problem of racial discrimination must be viewed . . . (for) discrimination against minority groups in the United States has an adverse effect upon our relations with other countries. Racial discrimination furnishes grist for the Communist propaganda mills, and it raises doubts even among friendly nations as to the intensity of our devotion to the democratic faith.[9]

How important were such arguments to the final outcome in *Brown v. Board?* No less an observer of the American racial scene than W.E.B. Du Bois expressed the view that "No such decision would have been possible without the . . . world pressure of Communism," which, he asserted, rendered it "simply impossible for the United States to continue to lead a 'Free World' with race segregation kept legal in more than a third of its territory."[10]

And to those for whom even an obvious truth has no validity unless whites embrace it, recourse to the news media coverage of the *Brown* decision should be helpful. After summing up the effect of the *Brown* decision on the children in the segregation states, *Time* magazine, observed: "The international effect may be scarcely less important. In many countries, where U.S. prestige and leadership have been damaged by the fact of U.S. segregation, it will come as a timely reassertion of the basic American principle that 'all men are created equal'."

Time's companion publication, *Life*, supported this position with the assertion that the Supreme Court "at one stroke immeasurably raised the respect of other nations for the U.S." And from *Newsweek* came these words: "the psychological effect will be tremendous . . . segregation in the public schools has become a symbol of inequality, not only to Negroes in the United States, but to colored peoples elsewhere in the world. It has also been a weapon of world Communism. Now that symbol lies shattered."

More pointed is the statement from *Citizen's Guide to Desegregation:* "The Voice of America carried the news around the world. Hundreds of national and international leaders wired congratulations. Only radio Moscow was silent."[11]

A final proof that the Supreme Court's decision to outlaw official racial apartheid was influenced, perhaps decisively, by the fear that Jim Crow policies might lead black people far less fortunate than Paul Robeson to follow his example, is found in the *Brown* opinion. Its pages contain no mention of the Communist menace, but cataloged the educational and emotional harm of segregated schools, decrying the damage done as so serious as to likely be irreparable. Then, assuming that open acknowledgement was as good as needed action, the Supreme Court deferred any remedy until the next year, at which time it decided that the entitlement of black children to attend desegregated schools need not be granted immediately, and might be delayed until administrative problems were solved—a deferential policy that lasted a full decade.

The Court's unprecedented deferral of a recognized constitutional right perfected a perfect parallel between *Brown* and the Emancipation Proclamation. Both documents were supposed to serve as a means of securing and advancing important interests of white society, and both condemned, in symbolic terms, obvious and long-standing racial injustice. Both actions were structured so as to mask the real benefits to whites behind assurances to the citizenry that the policy or decision is the tardy response to long-ignored petitions for racial reform. In fact, as Professor Mary L. Dudziak concluded, "efforts to promote civil rights within the United States were consistent with, and important to, the more central U.S. mission of fighting world communism.[12]

Even so, as most blacks accept such assurances without question, and, in both instances, mounted major movements (mass escapes in the nineteenth century and protests in the twentieth) that would have been effective even had no Proclamation or landmark decision prompted them. That blacks respond in this way is fortunate, because the Emancipation Proclamation—as indicated earlier—was unenforceable, and Brown's enforcement was delayed until blacks insisted on it.

By the time black protests and marches of the 1960s made Brown more than a symbol, Paul Robeson was on the sidelines, another in a long list of blacks sacrificed to the cause of racial equality in a land seemingly determined to destroy those who most believe in its ideals.

One wonders. What if Robeson were speaking out now? Even at the peak of his career, Paul Robeson at mid century did not command the massive celebrity enjoyed by some well-known blacks today. A national poll found that the three most popular Americans are black: retired General Colin Powell, Masters champion Tiger Woods, who is also part Asian, and basketball great Michael Jordan.[13] Their popularity spans across age, regional, professional, racial and political subgroups. They are better known among Democrats than President Clinton, and more popular among Republicans than House Speaker, Newt Gingrich. Powell, Woods, and Jordan are multimillionaires with income and wealth beyond anything Paul Robeson could have imagined.

Each of these men identifies with black Americans. Powell has voiced support for affirmative action and Woods has criticized the exclusionary practices of most private country clubs. Jordan does commercials for the Negro College Fund. What if these men emulated Paul Robeson and launched campaigns castigating America for the racism that most whites refuse to acknowledge and few blacks can escape? What if they called on whites to give up their privileges as whites and join with blacks for major social reforms needed by all? Would their celebrity-amplified voices move whites to explore the depth and breadth of racism that every black has experienced first-hand? Or, like Robeson, would the nation prefer to silence even these messengers—no matter their fame, wealth, and popularity?

For Robeson, these questions are less important than what he viewed as his obligation as an artist: to champion the cause of the oppressed. In his most famous stage role, Shakespeare's *Othello*, Paul Robeson says in the final stage, "I have done the state some small service. And they know it." Even today, that statement, applied to his life, would not be acknowledged by most Americans whose sense of security seems congenitally condemned to fear any black, particularly one whose achievements have been recognized and who then dares to criticize even the most odious racial problems.

Robeson's message to us is that in the face of adverse reaction, we must continue our protests against racial injustice. Despite the lessons of history, we hold open the door of fellowship to America's white masses when they discover, finally, that black people are not the cause and racism not the remedy for their oppression. We blacks may not save this country through such commitment, but we will save our souls, and we will have remained true to the rich testament Paul Robeson left us.

Justice Marshall and *The Handmaid's Tale*

Continued resistance by the powerless eventually triumphs over power, and thus oppression must be resisted, even when opposition seems useless.

Margaret Atwood's classic 1986 novel, *The Handmaid's Tale*, is a woman's story of triumph over travail and tragedy. In the 1980s, this woman had held an important position converting books into a computer database. She was, in addition, a wife and mother. She had a name. Now, she is Offred—a state-imposed label—and is a virtual prisoner in Gilead, a repressive, dictatorial, post-American regime centered on the campus of what had been Harvard University. Its rulers exercise absolute control over the citizenry. The penalty for even the least manifestation of heresy is a cruel death. The highly regimented masses have no rights and every aspect of life is set within narrow restrictions.[1]

Because of nuclear wars, pestilence, and pollution, encouraging Caucasian births has become a high government priority. Our heroine and many like her are pressed into service as subjugated breeders for the leaders whose wives are barren. Sexual intercourse is highly ritualized and carried out as described in the Old Testament story of Rachel gaining a child, fathered by her husband, Jacob, and borne by her maid, Bilhad.[2]

In Atwood's novel, Offred resorts to extraordinary

measures and takes enormous risks to retain her sanity and some remnants of her self-esteem. Because she is allowed no books or writing materials, she tries to remember all that she has experienced, all that she has endured. In the end, they take her away. Whether the guards are agents of the regime or persons in revolt against it, neither she nor the reader knows. At some point, though, beyond the story's ending, Offred records her life experiences and these recordings are discovered long years later.

Happily, we do not live in Margaret Atwood's "Gilead." Life is less than a picnic for persons of color in this land where whiteness is the deeply assumed norm. But it is not a totalitarian regime. Without fear of official censure or sanction, we can gather and offer commendations to black leaders who have served their people well. Some of these have been lawyers and judges, a group with the difficult task of disproving Audre Lorde's warning that one cannot dismantle the master's house with the master's tools.[3] When, at some far distant time, historians and anthropologists review the records of our era, there should be no mistake about them or the tremendous efforts they mounted to gain constitutional protection for our rights.

From our vantage point, these are heroes: lawyers, including Charles Houston, Haywood Burns, and the many courageous practitioners in the South who represented civil rights clients when it was both unpopular and dangerous to do so. Then there are the judges: William Hastie, Robert L. Carter, Constance Baker Motley, A. Leon Higginbotham, Bruce M. Wright and, the most revered of these, Associate Supreme Court Justice, Thurgood Marshall.[4]

Margaret Atwood's novel reminds us, though,

that time's perspectives are unpredictable. In her epilogue, anthropologists and other social scientists—all people of color—gather to share what they know about the long-dead Gilead regime. As with contemporary conferences, recreation plans and meal times hold a priority equal to that given the matters under discussion. At one session, an archivist describes a set of tapes, apparently those that Offred was able to record. Because details of interest to the scholars are not available, the archivist misconstrues, even trivializes the horrendous ordeal the tapes' author underwent. Finding Offred's identity uncertain, her fate unclear, the archivist expresses mild annoyance at the paucity of useful information contained in the tapes. Careful of the moderator's warning not to exceed his time, he closes his brief talk with an apology:

> As all historians know, the past is a great darkness, and filled with echoes. Voices may reach us from it; but what they say to us is imbued with the obscurity of the matrix out of which they come; and, try as we may, we cannot always decipher them precisely in the clearer light of our own day.[5]

The scholarly conference provides a frustrating and fearsome benediction to Atwood's novel. While the social scientists were disappointed that their questions about the character of the society remained unanswered, readers recognized that the true significance of the tapes was in their existence, not in what they contained. The scientists' misdirected inquiries sharpen rather than obscure our appreciation of the indomitable spirit of the woman who lived *The Handmaid's Tale*. She represents those in her time—and in all times—who strive to preserve their humanity while living in continuous misery, even at the risk of their lives. It is a commendable quality of spirit that is beyond effective commendation, nurtured as it must so often be in environments steeped in iniquities.

The confusion at the scholarly conference raises a question for us. Two centuries, hence, when researchers sift through the remnants of our records, will they both understand what we have said and—in that broader perspective available to them—will they uncover an unstated subtext to our commendations, one that may reflect fears that while unspoken, are no less real? We hail, for example, the great increase in the number of minority judges who now preside over courts at every level across this land. It is much too soon, though, to know whether these persons of color are truly pioneers of racial progress, or whether—as has happened in so many other areas of civil rights—they represent a temporary phenomenon fueled by factors and agents unconnected with and little mindful of their talents, their hard work, their courageous efforts to do justice. If the winds of perceived self-interest change, will those who come after us again be able to count the numbers of minority judges on the fingers of a single hand?

This was Offred's fate. For a woman who had seen the worst side of humanity, making the tapes was an extraordinary act of faith. Evidently, some part of her still believed that by telling what had happened to her, people would be moved to make sure it never happened again. But when we read the end of *The Handmaid's Tale*, we see that her trust was misplaced. The conference participants, who as scholars and people of color should have been best able to understand her message, are not moved by her story.

Does the fact that no one understands or praises the tapes diminish their importance as an act of defiance? I think not. Offred created, for herself and for us as readers, memory and identity in a land where both were obliterated. Perhaps most important to her character, she did what she believed was right and, in the process, took terrible risks and made sacrifices beyond anything she thought herself capable of doing.

Despite the accomplishments of minority judges, it is quite possible that, like Offred's tapes, their work will be misunderstood, even denigrated by future generations. When it comes to racial issues or individuals, this society has an amazing ability to alter its views chameleon-like to fit society's current need.

At Supreme Court Justice Thurgood Marshall's funeral, for example, speakers transformed the requiem into a celebration of a life committed to the eradication of racism. Borne on rhetorical wings, the eulogies lifted him to a place with Dr. Martin Luther King, Jr. in that uniquely American racial pantheon: Each man was accorded in death a distinction usually reserved for those who in life have achieved rather than failed to accomplish the goals for which they committed their lives.

This society readily assimilates the myriad manifestations of black protest and achievement. In that process, the continuing devastation wrought by racial discrimination is minimized, even ignored, while those who gained some renown as they worked to end those injustices are transformed into cultural reinforcements of the racial status quo. They become irrefutable proof that even minorities can make it in America through work and sacrifice. For some, it is easy then to conclude that those minorities who do not make it have only themselves to blame.

Though he denied it, many felt that Justice Marshall left the Court embittered by the dismantling of so many liberal precedents he had helped to establish. Marshall surely was not pleased as he witnessed conservative Court majorities dismantling decades of hard-won doctrine. A more probable source of bitterness was a tardy recognition that the reliance he and other civil rights advocates had placed in the law all too often served eventually as a betrayal of our clients and the masses of black people who relied on our counsel and willingly placed their hopes on our professional skill and commitment. He surely knew that, despite a lifetime of struggle and accomplishments that insured him a major place in American history, he—like many of us who tried to emulate him—believed we could effect racial reform through law. Too late, we discovered that the system distorted our commitment into co-optation, and transformed our advocacy of rights into doctrines of neutrally-imposed oppression.

We placed our civil rights advocacy in the service of our integrationist ideals, ignoring in the process our experience with the resiliency of racism. We viewed segregation as the prime barrier to black advancement. By our sustained efforts, we dismantled the hated "Jim Crow" signs, uncovering in the process the standards deemed "neutral" as to race, but that have developed into a more sophisticated and more invidious vehicle for maintaining white dominance.

Reversals in legal doctrine, combined with the devastating statistics of black poverty, unemployment, crime, and family and community destruction, are worsening so many lives despite the committed efforts of civil rights lawyers. And yet, we urged the use of law and litigation as the major means to end racial discrimination. We did so in good faith but with an inadequate understanding of both the limits of law and the pervasive role of racism in this society.

Like the character Offred in *The Handmaid's Tale*, Thurgood Marshall relied on the power of telling stories to change minds and events. In remarking on what Justice Marshall added to the Court, Justice Sandra Day O'Connor recalled in one interview his ability to use personal examples to convey the human realities behind the cold legal principles the Court debated. But like those at the conference who undervalued poor Offred's story, the Court's majority—and especially Justice O'Connor whose votes and opinions committing the Court to a nonexistent color-blind society have helped demolish so many civil rights precedents—was unable to get beyond the humor In Justice Marshall's anecdotes to his deeply serious messages—now relegated to his dissenting opinions.

We who honor Marshall continue to labor in the legal vineyards, hoping our efforts—whether in the courtroom or in the classroom—can relieve racism's burdens. It is distracting though to realize that Marshall's successor on the Supreme Court seems to personify a well-traveled road to success for minorities. Namely, if we ignore the continuing perversity of racism and act as though the law is fair and color-blind, those who grant positions and prestige will reward our conformance with their rose-colored assumptions. Perhaps Justice Clarence Thomas' true value to people of color—particularly legal professionals—is that his presence provides us with a constant reminder that what many of us condemn as a serious deficiency in him is, as well, a constant temptation to us all.

The historic pattern of extolling the system while

blaming the victims of that system is neither a new nor fortuitous phenomenon. Robert L. Allen in his 1969 book, *Black Awakening in Capitalist America*, reminds us that what we deem as progress measured by the number of blacks who have moved into management-level positions, is quite similar to developments in colonial Africa and India. The colonizing countries maintained their control by establishing class divisions within the ranks of the indigenous peoples. A few able (and safe) individuals were permitted to move up in the ranks where they served as false symbols of what was possible for the subordinated masses. In this, and less enviable ways, these individuals provide a legitimacy to the colonial rule that it clearly did not deserve. Allen's point is summarized by a social scientist in *The Handmaid's Tale* who observes that "no empire imposed by force or otherwise has ever been without this feature: control of the indigenous by members of their own group."[6]

In his gruff, plain-spoken way, Justice Marshall recognized and resented this role. He once told an audience at his alma mater, Howard University:

> [People tell me] "You ought to go around the country and show yourself to Negroes; and give them inspiration." For what? Negro kids are not fools. They know when you tell them there is a possibility that someday you'll have a chance to be the o-n-l-y Negro on the Supreme Court, those odds aren't too good.[7]

Judge Constance Baker Motley, a civil rights colleague of Justice Marshall who herself has served for many years on the federal district court, also understands the limits of our acceptance and both the consequences and the opportunities inherent in our special status. Shortly after she joined the court, Judge Motley was asked why so many tough, Vietnam-era protest cases came to her court—as opposed to those of her white colleagues, particularly when her courageous rulings were often reversed on appeal. She replied, simply: "When you are in the club, you want to stay in the club. But, if you were never in the club, never expect to be in the club, you are free to do what needs to be done."

Writer Robert Allen defines the dimensions of the club. He views Black America as a domestic colony of White America. Colonial rule, Allen claims, is predicated upon "an alliance between the occupying power and indigenous forces of conservatism and tradition." Allen finds aspects of this policy in American slavery where slave owners created divisions between field hands and house hands. "Uncle Tom," is the term used to describe the collaborator torn, with conflicting loyalties, between his people and the slave owners.

We cannot escape the burden of Allen's analysis, nor should we wish to. The oppression that challenges people of color and those with the status as law professionals is less violent and dominating than that described in Atwood's, *The Handmaid's Tale*, but it is not less real or potentially less destructive. Both Justice Marshall and Judge Motley understand the dilemma in Allen's analysis. They, like many of us, relish our positions because they offer an opportunity to push the legal system, and maybe even the larger society, in the direction of racial justice. Our involvement, though, may be having a very different effect than we hope or even recognize. Instead of gaining access to real influence, it is more likely that we are legitimizing a system that relegates us to an ineffectual but decorative fringe. Offred, with all her humiliations, recognizes that she is better off than many, a privileged status she describes in graphic terms. "I have enough daily bread, so I won't waste my time on that. It isn't the main problem. The problem is getting it down without choking on it."[8]

And what of those minorities less fortunate than ourselves? We unintentionally can make things worse instead of better for minorities who have been excluded from the programs which have helped us to gain skills and acceptable credentials. Enjoying our positions and the occasional opportunity to do good, we are pointed out to the majority of blacks who are still without work or trapped in low wage dead-end jobs. We want to serve as models for the disadvantaged, but as scholars, judges and practitioners, we are for many whites, "living proof that there is no color bar." The commander in Gilead to whom Offred is assigned would be surprised at such carping, as he is surprised to learn that the handmaids are not happy in their new "better" world: "Better," he concedes, "never means better for everyone. It always means worse, for some."[9]

The statement represents utilitarian thinking at a particularly fearful level. Perhaps out of their fear, there is a tendency for both some blacks along with some out-group whites to identify with those whites higher on the ladder, rather than feeling an allegiance to those poor Blacks who face similar obstacles. This attraction by both blacks and whites to whites with power facilitates an acceptance of injustices. In *The Handmaid's Tale*, Margaret Atwood describes a class of working men who, like American whites, are denied most of the privileges that come with money and power. They do not challenge the system, but like so many in our own day, they dream only of obtaining the perks of those in power.

Because the mesh of racism is so woven into the nation's essential fabric, I am convinced we can never eradicate it. There is only conduct based on a commitment to challenge it at every turn, at every new variation. Justice Marshall made this point in what was to be almost his last major speech. He said: "[t]he battle for racial and economic justice is not yet won; indeed, it has barely begun."[10]

Marshall gave vent to yearnings that we all share. He said:

> I wish I could say that racism and prejudice were only distant memories . . . and that liberty and equality were just around the bend. I wish I could say that America has come to appreciate diversity and to see and accept similarity.
>
> But as I look around, I see not a nation of unity but of division—afro and white, indigenous and immigrant, rich and poor, educated and illiterate.[11]

Justice Marshall warned that there is no sanctuary in the suburbs. "We cannot play ostrich. Democracy cannot flourish amid fear. Liberty cannot bloom amid hate. Justice cannot take root amid rage."[12]

Rather, Marshall urged continued confrontation with the evils he had fought all of his professional life. No promise of victory here, no guarantee of success. He called us to the need and to the sense of salvation inherent in struggle for struggle's sake.

> We must go against the prevailing wind. We must dissent from indifference. We must

dissent from apathy. We must dissent from the fear, the hatred and the mistrust. We must dissent from a government that has left its young without jobs, education, or hope. We must dissent from the poverty of vision and the absence of moral leadership. We must dissent because America can do better, because America has no choice but to do better.[13]

One of our responsibilities is to cultivate our awareness of what our roles are and what our histories have been. Like the handmaid, we must struggle to preserve our memories of the "time before." Offred hoped her tapes would remind the future that there was another way of living and that future generations would not accept oppression simply because they could not envision a choice. Our not so distant recollections of the overt barriers to black success and dignity are equally important. Not because, as in the handmaid's case, they show us who we can be, but because they remind us what we must not allow ourselves to become again.

The Handmaid's Tale warns us that even those gains we consider rock-solid can be taken away in a moment. While it would be hard to imagine that anyone could force us to give up the still-limited equality we have won, the kingdom of Gilead scares us because some part of us recognizes that it is not so fantastical. Although less dramatic, the last decade has shown us that we cannot rely on the pleasant but naive belief that, having been set in motion, our society and our progress in it will continue forward.

Justice Marshall is right about the crisis we face as a nation. Most of the nation, though, including many of its economic victims who are not black, does not see it that way. The storm clouds on the horizon representing joblessness, decreasing opportunity, increasing disparities in income and wealth, all of these clouds and more point to future calamities that people of color must suffer but that we did not cause. Justice Marshall's admonition to continue the struggle is, of course, no less appropriate because there are so many signs that struggle does not guarantee success. The moral of *The Handmaid's Tale* is that there can be triumph through struggle, even when that struggle ends in seeming defeat. We hail Justice Marshall and the heroine of Margaret Atwood's novel, not because they won, but because they persevered.

The Black Sedition Papers

The courage to confront racism, while worthy of praise, should not obscure the fact that the powerful can employ our confrontative statements to serve their ends as effectively as they can those deplorable self-blaming comments by blacks.

"We haven't given much attention to black scholars, a group whose numbers have increased in the last few decades. Through their writings, lectures, and television appearances, some of them have more influence on public opinion and policy-making than do all but the top, Black elected officials. And yet, while Black academics are viewed as spokespersons for the race, they are neither elected by blacks nor held accountable to them."

"We might as well tell it all, Geneva. Black scholars gain our positions through the tenure process. This fact translates into a not so subtle pressure to take positions in our writing that will not upset the mostly white faculty and college administration who hire and promote us. It goes without saying that those doing the selecting tend to be attracted to minority candidates who appear as much like them as possible, and are most happy if the minority person's research and writing are comforting rather than confrontative."

"Well, thankfully," Geneva observed generously, "what white faculty members want is not always what they get."

"No, what they get is often what they need: minority faculty members who will provide a different perspective on law, on life. Even so, no matter the value, many academics view our scholarly efforts as worthless because we depart from the norm, namely, how the white guys do it."

"So how did you escape the demand for confor- mance? Early on in my teaching career, I asked a senior colleague what he and others on the faculty considered good scholarly writing. He responded with a rather patronizing grin and told me we would have to discuss it sometime. At that moment, I understood how the guy must have felt when in response to his question, 'what is jazz,' the great jazz trumpeter Louis Armstrong responded: 'Man, if you don't know, don't mess with it.' I never asked again. Actually, it was liberating. I decided to write what I wanted to write in ways I thought would communi- cate my ideas and experiences."

"With my help, of course."

"Of course, Geneva. But it doesn't end there. We academics have access to public platforms—particu- larly those of us with ideas or expertise in the race area. We all want our work to be accepted rather than ignored. So, it's quite tempting to write and say what whites want to hear rather than what most blacks believe."

"The obvious question. What if the black acade- mic actually believes what will be comforting to whites?"

"That is precisely the question that one black professor posed during one of our many discussions on the subject. I urged not self-censorship, but restraint."

"He didn't see the difference, right?"

"It's a concept easier to understand than articu- late, Geneva. When I joined the Justice Department right out of law school, I worked with Maceo Hubbard, then one of the few black lawyers in Justice and a man with a lot of wisdom based on long experience. When I told him I was writing a letter of recommendation for a friend, he gave me some valuable advice that I've never forgotten. Maceo said: 'When you write that letter to the white folks for your black friend, keep this in mind: You can hurt him, but you can't help him.'"

Geneva laughed. "It's sad, but true. You can shout the merits of blacks to the four winds and get only a deafening silence in return. But whisper some criticism, and the society is suddenly all ears. You are in the spotlight, in demand for all the talk shows. It must be hard to resist, particularly if you really believe what you are saying."

"Often, though, it is a truth without context. If I say that one-third of young black men are incarcerated or caught up in the criminal justice system, it's true. But without the context of why they are where they are, it is easy for whites to draw the conclusion that all those young black men are right where they belong."

"Didn't your friend, the Rev. Peter Gomes, offer you some insight on what some black academics see as a dilemma?"

"He did. As minister of the Memorial Church at Harvard, he spoke at a dinner black students gave me before I left to become dean at the Oregon Law School. It is the key to what I view as the obligation of black people in positions where our voices can be heard by broad segments of the public. He warned me that as a dean, you are an evil. For you will have authority and sometimes you will unwittingly use that authority to disappoint expectations you should reward and will reward those expectations you should disappoint. There is no way you can avoid such unintended mischief. So, each morning upon arising, you must look at yourself in the mirror, and remind yourself, 'I am a dean and thus I am an evil.' Then you must ask, 'but today, can I be a necessary evil?'[1]

"It didn't take me long to learn that Gomes was sadly wrong about the authority available—for either good or mischief—to a law school dean. But his admonition is most appropriate for successful blacks whose very success is used to make life harder for the many blacks whom they would like to help. For all of us, each day provides another opportunity to become, as Rev. Gomes would put it, "a necessary evil." That is, we must not become so caught up in career advancement that we fail either to remember ourselves or remind those in authority that our individual advancement is not synonymous with group progress. Any number of those stranded in so-called ghetto pathology not only look like us, they —but for our good fortune and their lack of same—would be us. Our basic challenge must be to act in ways that alleviate their suffering, if we can, and to strive not to make it worse."

"Sound advice, friend, but there is a Sisyphean element that is missing from your current formulation. Your rather strong critique of a piece by Harvard Professor Orlando Patterson tried to explore this. His article was titled *Blacklash: The Crisis of Gender Relations among African Americans.*[2] Your response began by wondering—for whom does Patterson write? But I think your piece places in context our discussion about black academics, and provides a disturbing answer to your question: for whom do black academics speak?"[3]

ೲೲೲ

In *Blacklash*, Orlando Patterson reviews the dire plight of African American men, both those the society has already stamped "unwanted, unneeded, and obsolete," and those who, despite a modicum of success, live with the often unhappy manifestations of the fear that they, too, are endangered.

Professor Patterson delineates multiple forms of self-destructive behavior and traces their likely origins to slavery and a still-persistent racism. And yet there is an accusatory tone that implies that black men must somehow pull themselves up and find the power to function as good middle class citizens, despite the society's hostility. Who among us does not wish for such a miracle of transformation?

Given government's failure to intervene in any significant way other than build more prisons and hire more police, we must conceive and carry out a massive form of self-help in the psychological as well as the economic and political areas. *Blacklash*, though, is painfully long on admonition and pathetically short on plans or programs. As for psychological rebirth, Patterson condemns a "new man" model as so much "Afrocentric mumbo-jumbo." He cites with approval Franz Fanon's statement that "Revolution begins with the self, in the self," but there is nothing in Patterson's article suggesting a spiritual rebirth through commitment to the kind of revolution that Fanon urged.[4] Patterson urges a "cold turkey" antidote for racism's poison, which sounds hollow. Black condemnation without context. It is easy to predict that many whites will hail *Blacklash* publicly as courageous and absorb it because it's comforting. Blacks will likely find the article deeply troubling and condemn it as one more burden to bear.

I have not made a practice of publicly questioning the writings of Professor Patterson or other black scholars with whom I disagree. And, I am sure he expects his *Blacklash* paper to generate a storm of protest from blacks, particularly black women in the arms of whose criticism Patterson seems to glow.[5] I am moved to add my objections because of a letter I received from another black scholar, one who has devoted his career to examining government agencies that operate secretly.

Dear Professor:

No one in authority is willing to acknowledge that the studies are underway. The sponsors are unknown and funding for the project emanates from sources free of Congressional oversight. The purpose of the studies, if persistent rumors are accurate, is so controversial that secrecy is understandable—if hardly more justifiable. According to my sources, social instability in the black community is alarming policy-makers at the highest levels. All concede that blacks have survived hundreds of years of societal hostility and, in the process, have exhibited amazing resilience in the face of oppressive racial policies ranging from slavery to segregation.

Today, however, many blacks are experiencing unprecedented and precipitous declines that pose a national security risk. To meet this danger, the nation has so increased penalties for criminal conduct that an ever increasing number of blacks are either in prison or are enmeshed in the criminal justice system. Even so, the leaders of this project believe the society must be prepared to accept measures that circumvent due process and other constitutional safeguards.

The genesis of this racial crisis can be summarized easily. The ending of legally enforced segregation led many blacks to assume that desegregation laws would be enforced with the same vigor as their segregation predecessors. They were not. Indeed, much to the amazement of those who had worked long and hard for their enactment, civil rights laws intended to protect blacks from discriminatory practices are interpreted by courts and policy makers to bar programs intended to remedy decades of discrimination.

In addition, long-established stabilizing forces in the black community weakened as better-prepared blacks moved into mainly white work sites, schools, neighborhoods—even churches. Massive unemployment, referred to euphemistically as "down-sizing," has decimated black and white workers, but the impact on blacks has been particularly devastating. The result is apparent in the destabilization of families and communities and the tremendous increase in antisocial behavior.

Given these developments, the secret project leaders decided to quietly commission a series of "black sedition papers." These papers will record the effects on blacks of late twentieth-century economic, political, and social disadvantage. Under the ground rules, the papers are to focus on black pathology, describing it in detail and condemning those afflicted with it. Whenever possible, the studies will inject self-help solutions criticizing blacks for not thinking of and adopting these solutions themselves.

Except as asides, the studies do not place any responsibility on the society's racism for the black pathologies under examination. Investigators are urged not to "muddy the waters" by suggesting that black conduct is in any significant degree the result of environmental forces including particularly, white racism. Comparisons of negative behaviors of blacks with similar conduct by other oppressed groups is frowned on. On the other hand, writers are encouraged to make uncomplimentary analogies of black failure with the greater coping mechanisms by other disadvantaged peoples. West Indian immigrants are a favored comparison group. Successes by Asians, Hispanics, and Jews are also welcomed.

The project gathers studies by a diverse array of individuals and groups. Black social scientists, though, are preferred for reasons that seem to elude those blacks who are selected. The public's responses to these "black papers" are carefully followed and recorded. It is important that if the racial crisis worsens and authoritarian measures are called for, the public will be prepared.

Sincerely,

D.M.S., Ph.D.

I cannot say for a fact that Professor Orlando Patterson's *Blacklash* article is one of the "black sedition papers." To confirm my suspicions, I tried to contact my friend to find out more about these papers. He had not mentioned any of the scholars the secret project commissioned to write for them. And, yet, in trying to understand why he would write a paper that so distorts black history and contemporary black distress, it is reasonable to raise questions and, perhaps, hope for answers. Consider:

Even the title is accusatory. "Backlash," in contemporary usage, often refers to the strong negative reaction by whites to civil rights remedies they think go too far. *Blacklash* suggests that blacks are turning against one another and thus are primarily responsible for growing opposition to civil rights in general and blacks in particular. In fact, racial policies in this country have very little to do with black "worthiness" and everything to do with the perception of what will best serve white interests. Justice Clarence Thomas' appointment fit the Republican political agenda. That being the case, it was irrelevant that he lacked the usual qualifications for the Supreme Court, and additionally was accused of conduct that fits the fearsome, black male stereotype.

On the other hand, there is virtually no political support to address the roots of black crime even though fear of black crime has helped elect presidents. Crime also serves as sufficient justification for massive funding programs for those who construct prisons or work in them. Crime and most other issues of deviant behavior are far more political—read economic—than moral problems. Professor Patterson's failure to address this basic reality is fatal to a paper that—whatever his intentions—will harm more black folks than it will help.

Patterson, using the Anita Hill-Clarence Thomas debacle—a topic he has explored before[6] —weaves a destructive image of the relationship between black men and women in a society where, he claims, blacks have gained "final acceptance . . . as integral—even if still greatly disadvantaged—members of the society." He explains that the Hill-Thomas hearings were symbolic of blacks as accepted members of society. Patterson says that Anita Hill and Clarence Thomas are more importantly a man and woman who just happen to be black. And the relationship or lack of it that existed between them is no different than the relationship that exists between white males and females.

It is tempting to join Professor Patterson in reaching for any slight evidence that the increasingly heavy burden of racism is easing, but the hearings were not that. I think it safe to say that most black people in America—with the exception of Professor Patterson—were continuously and painfully aware of the race of the two protagonists and many of their witnesses. Had Anita Hill been white and Clarence Thomas' wife black, the questioning of both—and likely the outcome of the hearings—would have been very, very different.

In the gender debate the hearings generated, Anita Hill, Patterson claims, was a symbolic figure for white women as well as black women. Here, his racial optimism ignores black history. Campaigns for racial justice have often been used as a vehicle by other groups to further their own advances. And though those groups make progress toward their goals due to black people, they continue to hold racist views. In the beginning of the women's suffrage movement, women and blacks fought together. Frederick Douglass and Susan B. Anthony often campaigned together in order to get legislation passed that would give both groups access to the ballot. But, when it appeared that black men would receive the right to vote before white women, Anthony and other white women quickly dropped all ties with blacks. Some early feminists even went so far as to insinuate to white men that black people were not human and, thus, how could they [white men] possibly think about giving blacks the ballot before their own white women. Consider, as well, the exploitation of racial issues by both political parties in national elections over the last twenty years.

On the dubious evidence of the Thomas-Hill hearings, Patterson envisions an American landscape swept clean of the "culture of slavery" though he concedes that "its legacies are still very much with us." Asserting that blacks are no longer outsiders concentrating on getting in, Patterson writes that we must focus on the top of the "internal racial agenda. . .the crisis-ridden problem of gender relations between African American men and women." *Blacklash* is filled with "there is racism, but" statements that acknowledge the racist source of the problems Patterson describes, but he refuses to find them the prime factor in the behavioral patterns he deplores. Instead, Patterson points to black women in general and black feminists in particular as the cause of a crisis, one he asserts would be more obvious if black feminists were not obscuring our understanding of gender relations by insisting that they bear a double burden based on race and gender.

Patterson believes that close examination of the life experiences and social relationships of the two sexes within white dominant society, reveals that African American men, not women, are at the bottom of the well. In order to invalidate the "double burden theory" of African American women, Patterson depicts a grim picture for African American men and an encouraging picture for African American women. He states that in some instances, black women are in better economic position than white women by historically tracing the black woman's ability to gain entry into the dominant white world. This entry, Patterson feels, allowed black women a chance to experience "finer things in life" and an opportunity to develop relationships with their white counterparts.

Patterson cites statistics showing higher education attainment and income for African American females as compared to black males to support his position that the life chances of black males are worse than those of black females. Furthermore, Patterson argues that the economic status of black women is not only better than their male counterparts, but cites data intended to show that in many circumstances, they have surpassed their white female counterparts. Her enviable position is primarily rooted in the fact that white men do not find black women attractive or regard them as "women" as they would white females. This unattractiveness, Patterson claims, shield black women from sexual oppression by white men. Therefore black women, Patterson states, exist in a small crevice, better than white women, not higher than white men, but sufficiently better "that black professional men tend to get crushed."

Patterson continues this exercise in high-wire reasoning without apparent worry about the absence of a safety net of supporting fact or experience by tracing the history of black women in this country. His account of slavery, like much of his writing, is plagued with a kind of half-sight. Because enslaved women could bear children and thereby increase their worth as property, they were valued by slave owners. Patterson, though, viewed this economic benefit as giving slave women an ability to "pass" within white society.

Patterson then claims that after slavery a black woman's ability to pass was augmented because she performed work as a domestic, nanny, nurse or clerk. These positions, he states, allowed black women "greater access to the wider dominant white world." Service sector employment brought black and white women together to share close relationships. Unfortunately, black men, due to their sex and inability to bear children, could not pass into the white world. In fact, black men could not obtain employment which would allow a relationship to grow between them and their white counterparts.

The evidence contrary to this position is enormous. Professor Cheryl Harris' article, "Whiteness as Property,"[7] provides a dramatic instance with its story of how her fair-skinned grandmother literally "passed" for white in order to obtain a clerk's position in a downtown Chicago department store. Harris' grandmother, having gained entry into the white dominant society in order to support her family, "listened to the women with whom she worked discuss their worries, their children's illnesses, their husbands' disappointments, their boyfriends' infidelities—all of the mundane yet critical things that made up their lives. She came to know them but they did not know her, for" as Professor Harris explains, "my grandmother occupied a completely different place. That place—where white supremacy and economic domination meet—was unknown turf to her white co-workers." Entry into the dominant world by black women in order to support their families has seldom been the fabled crystal stair that Patterson has created.

Black women seeking careers in law teaching will also wish to differ with Patterson. Studies show they have had a disproportionately hard time gaining entry into law school faculties, compared with black men.[8] Their numbers on faculties at Harvard University are ludicrously small, a fact that Patterson overlooks out of either misplaced loyalty or an acceptance of the Harvard line that "we simply can't find any who are qualified." According to one study, Harvard University, where there are only 80 blacks of 4,842 faculty members (1.7%), will require until the year 2072 to reach the national average of black faculty (4.5%), if it continues at its present pace—five new, black faculty members in seven years.[9] At present, no more than two or three of the tenured blacks at Harvard are women.

Even in the marketplace, black women face disadvantages. A survey of new car dealer pricing practices revealed that black women are charged more for the same vehicle than either white men and women, and more than black men.[10]

Given the widely held belief that competitive market forces will eliminate racial and gender discrimination, and that such discrimination will occur only in markets in which racial or gender animus distorts competition, the car dealer study reveals double-bound bias with a special vengeance. My point here is not to engage in a battle of studies, but to illustrate that the assumption that black women have an easier time in this society than black men cannot be proved. Its assertion as gospel is divisive in a gender setting already beset with external pressures due to a racism Patterson would have us believe is no longer a primary factor.

Slavery may have, as Patterson insists, left an indelible mark on African American women and men. And those scars may have affected our ability to create and sustain meaningful relationships with one another. The question is the degree to which contemporary manifestations of racism affect and sustain these scars of oppression. Indeed, to what degree do divisive aspects of the society that lead to high divorce rates among whites also tend to separate black couples—or, interracial couples for that matter?

There is absolutely no doubt that black men are in a state of emergency, with more black men in prison than in college, fewer black men receiving higher education than black women. And, there is little doubt that some employers see black women as capable of better fulfilling affirmative action obligations because they occupy dual positions as blacks and women. The debate, though, should not focus on whether black men or black women have been affected most by hostile white society and the steadily deteriorating labor market. Rather, our efforts should be focused on why black men are suffering a genocide-like demise from the work-force, from the family and, increasingly, from life itself. This tragedy has affected black women deeply. They, after all, are the mothers, wives, and sisters of America's "Disappeared." It is only when we observe the black man and woman in unison rather than individually, that we can fully understand the plight of African Americans.

In a survey conducted by *Ebony* magazine among African Americans,[11] 43.5% of the respondents felt that relations between the men and women are improving. But, 26.2% males and 29% females who responded believed that relations are getting worse. The respondents felt that "the root cause [of the division between black men and women] is the socioeconomic environment that penalizes black men and engenders suspicion between black men and women."[12] How can it be that what is so obvious to *Ebony*'s readers is lost on an academic of Professor Patterson's stature?

No one will disagree with Professor Patterson when he asserts that black people must assist ourselves. Such urging, though, coming from one writing from the safe haven of the academy harms rather than helps when it claims that a segment of our community is without morals, values, and feelings as though these all too obvious deficits occurred without an external cause or that they can be corrected without a reversal of social policies that now sustain conditions and motivate behaviors that we all deplore. Shifting the root cause from a hostile society to black women is both inaccurate in fact and counter productive to the self-help goal Patterson espouses. The only predictable result is reinforcement of a belief in even some liberal whites that blacks are genetically predisposed to antisocial life patterns. Secure in this unspoken view, policy-making whites are freed of any obligation for even thinking about, much less funding, expensive new programs of social reconstruction.

At this point, I planned to end my critique by urging Professor Patterson and other academics to remember that we not only enjoy a degree of academic freedom that protects our writings from retaliatory censor, but also that our writing garners a degree of attention far greater than anything the masses we are deemed to speak for can equal. Given our representative role for the black community, whether we want it or not, it is appropriate that when discussing racial issues, we adopt a basic precept of physicians: "First, do no harm."

After all, when we attack those responsible for and profiting from racism's continued virulence, those we accuse are not without either the power or the will to respond. But when we aim our assaults at a people whose dire predicament is without precedent in a history that includes 200 years of slavery, then there is an ethical obligation to consider our positions in the light of the likely use of our words by those who despise and are quite willing to see dead a segment of our people who—after all—look like us, however different they may act. As Cornel West made clear in reporting an incident with New York taxis that most of us have experienced,[13] our looks for many whites are conclusive—regardless of our educational, cultural, and even financial attainments.

Must we then remain silent about serious short-comings and self-defeating activities in black communities? Of course, not. We need no black Daniel Moynihans bemoaning that they have been crucified on a cross of truth about ghetto pathologies. But Moynihan's critics were not afraid of the truth. The issue, Professor Stephen Steinberg contends,[14] "concerns the theoretical claims that are advanced concerning the causes of these well-known afflictions, together with the related issue of what is to be done about them." Inclusion of causes as well as effects is essential to counteract the presumption of unworthiness that translates the failings of a subordinated people into self-caused fault rather than an externally-imposed fate.

After completing my response, I received a message from my academic friend investigating Black Sedition Papers. Again, I share his letter with you.

 оюоюою

Dear Professor:

I received your message. I have two pieces of information that you will be interested in. First, I can confirm your suspicions. Professor Orlando Patterson's *Blacklash* article is considered a Black Sedition Paper. It will be quietly circulated to policymakers as evidence of both the hopelessness of the black condition, and blacks' inability or unwillingness to take the strong, moral steps needed to continue as productive members of the society. I found no evidence that Patterson was commissioned to write this paper, or that he has received any direct compensation for its publication. Indeed, I found no evidence that he is even aware of how his paper will be used.

Second, I have learned that the Black Sedition Paper files contain a number of writings that are as unremittingly harsh in their assessments of whites and racism as you claim Professor Patterson is heartless in his assessment of black people. This group of quite militant papers actually supplements their more conservative counterparts. It is expected that, when it is time to invoke them, the militant and conservative papers together will be used to convince a larger spectrum of the white population of the need for draconian measures against all blacks.

I understand that the militant files contain a number of your writings.

Sincerely,
D.M.S.

Bluebeard's Castle: An American Fairy Tale

Life seems to favor those in power, while it seldom rewards with triumph and good works. The righteous must rely on their faith, champion truth and justice even in a seemingly lost cause.

*B*luebeard's Castle[1] is a French fairy tale about a nobleman who marries a succession of women, escorts them to his castle where they disappear and are never heard from again.[2] The Hungarian composer, Bela Bartok, working from a variation of the story, composed a darkly beautiful opera about Bluebeard's fourth wife, Judith, who ignores her family's warnings and marries the strange and awe-inspiring man whose great power she hopes to humanize with her devotion, with her love.[3]

Bartok's opera is stark. Even though written in 1911, the harmonies sound strange and dissonant; symbolism fills both text and music. We know at the outset that Judith is doomed and yet she intrigues us with the increasingly dangerous risks she takes to fulfill her vision of her ideal life with Bluebeard. As she urges him to provide her with an openness he is unable to give, there appears a parallel with the plight of black Americans, a revelatory perspective from which to review the unkept promises of racial justice made to black people throughout American History.

Upon entering his foreboding, windowless fortress, Judith realizes that the sun can never enter. The walls are not simply musty but wet.[4] She sings ominously:

> *Darkness rules within your castle.*
> *Oozing waters! Bluebeard, tell me.*
> *Can it be that stone is weeping?*
> *Can a castle feel its sadness?*

Along the somber corridor she detects seven locked doors and, seeking light and some understanding of her husband's life, she urges Bluebeard to allow her to open all of them:

> *That the stone be done with weeping,*
> *That the air once more be live,*

He refuses, urging her to accept him on faith and not look behind the doors:

> *Life you are and light, my Judith.*
> *Love me, trust me, ask me nothing.*

Judith knows that in the midst of devastation, neither love nor life can be sustained on unearned trust. Despite the ominous signs, she wants to believe her marriage will succeed. Surely, the symbols of reassurance for happiness and acceptance she seeks must lie behind those doors. With great effort, Judith gains from Bluebeard one key at a time. She opens each door in expectation, but finds increasingly horrifying sustenance for her fears. Bluebeard's torture weapons are in one chamber, his armaments, his gold, and his jewels are in another. One door opens to a scene of his vast land holdings, another to a beautiful flower garden. Each scene, however, is stained with blood.

Bluebeard declares his love for his newest wife and urges her not to unlock the seventh door.

Judith, her hope gone, and expecting the worse, nevertheless insists on opening that door. In a haunting aria she sings:

> *Now I know what waits behind it,*
> *Now I know its fatal secret! Blood is on your gems*
> *and weapons;*
> *Blood besmears your flower garden;*
> *Over your domain's expanses Blood encroaches like*
> *a shadow.*
> *Now I know whose tears of sorrow*
> *Fill the lake with mournful silence:*
> *There lie all your former wives,*
> *They lie in blood, the blood of murder!*
> *Woe! How true were my forebodings!*

With trembling hands Judith opens the final door. Inside stand Bluebeard's three former wives. He has not murdered them. Rather, they are living, very beautiful, but quite pale as they advance in single file, splendidly adorned with mantles, crowns, and jewels.

Bluebeard approaches Judith. Despite her pleas for mercy, he arrays her, as the others, with a mantle, crown, and jewels. Sadly, she follows her predecessors through the door which closes after her. The stage darkens. The curtain falls.

❧❧❧

The fairy tale, as analyzed in a study of that literary genre by Robert Darnton,[5] is far more than an amusing narrative for children. Originating from folktales, fairy tales did not always have happy endings, but primarily reflected the harsh experiences of the peasants' lives. The peasant versions "undercut the notion that virtue will be rewarded or that life can be conducted according to any principle other than basic mistrust."[6] Surely, the oppressive experiences of American blacks, so much a part of the Spirituals, the Blues, and Gospel music, are not unlike the harsh existence of early eighteenth-century French peasants, as reflected in their fairy tales.

I know of no exact parallels in American folk literature to Bluebeard who sought to find in a new wife a symbol through which he might extirpate his evil past. His goal eludes him, however, because Judith, try as she might to become the instrument of his liberation, is unable to move him beyond his desire for dominance. Her commitment to him is insufficient because only Bluebeard can take the step that could bring sunlight to his castle, salvation to his soul.

That step, the transformation of corruptive power for cooperative sharing is analogous to American society which periodically produces a symbol of redemption in the wake of unspeakable cruelty or crippling racial discrimination. At the national level, the symbol is usually a policy with liberating potential: the Emancipation Proclamation,[7] the post-Civil War Amendments,[8] the decision in *Brown v. Board of Education*, the Civil Rights Acts of 1964,[9] the Voting Rights Act of 1965, and, of course, the Affirmative Action Movement. Actually, there are many more lesser ones, but these six policies, while fashioned out of the honest commitment of some and the selfish self-interest of many, contain the potential to expunge this nation's Bluebeard image: the dark stain of slavery and racism. Without looking closely at the motives behind these long-sought policies, black Americans have accepted the language of their redemptive promise and have urged their fulfillment. Like Judith, they have urged white America to:

Let in sunlight, light completely
Flood the darkness from your castle,
Let the Breeze in! Let the sun in!
Soon, O soon,
The air itself will ring with blessings!

After much effort, a door is opened, but after a brief period of hope, blacks again find themselves trapped in the darkness of a new and more subtle set of subordinating social shadows. They cry out in petition and prayer for the light of racial justice. For many, despair is displayed in antisocial, self-destructive behavior. Society's response can be summarized in Bluebeards answer to Judith who pleaded that he let in the wind, the sun, the light.

Nothing can enlight this castle.

If the contemporary economic distress of so many black Americans represented the first time their expectations had been dashed by conditions over which they possessed no control, it would still be no less a disaster. As with any natural catastrophe, one would at least expect that nature's devastation would not strike the same place time and time again. History indicates, though, that from the very beginning, the subordination of blacks has been tied at least as closely to economic factors as it has been to the deeply-held belief in white superiority.[10] Indeed, the latter belief, functioning in the face of the most basic biological facts, is nurtured and sustained by a fertilization process that is economic rather than intellectual.

As Bluebeard's wives were doomed to suffer imprisonment, blacks seem foreordained to endure one racial disaster after another. The tableau changes with the times, but its structure and final outcome remain constant. Each reconciliation is a wedding feast, rich with exchanged promises of freedom for blacks and forgiveness for whites. Forgiving and extending themselves in reliance on the promises of a new day, blacks discover all too soon that the new relationship, while seeming better than the one they risked so much to escape, has placed them in a different but still subordinate posture. Each time, the symbol of the new relationship ends up behind a new and more imposing door, constructed of current economic needs and secured with a racism that is no less efficient because some blacks are able to slip by the barriers of class, wealth and bigotry.

Using the idiom of *Bluebeard's Castle*, let us examine the carnage of hopes beyond six doors, each of which—until opened—held out the promise of black freedom.

DOOR I. THE EMANCIPATION PROCLAMATION

When Abraham Lincoln signed the Executive Order purporting to free the slaves in Confederate-held territory, it electrified the world and ensured that the North would triumph in the Civil War. Responding to the Emancipation order with unbounded enthusiasm, slaves disrupted southern work forces, destroying property, and escaping in ever-swelling numbers. Nearly 200,000 blacks enlisted in the Union Army and made the decisive difference for the North in many battlefield victories.

Although the Emancipation Proclamation, bolstered by the thirteenth amendment, undermined the legal claims of slave masters, it created no substantive rights in the slaves themselves. The freedom document left them defenseless against resubjugation under the notorious Black Codes, race riots, and widespread white terror and intimidation.[11] Congress, for its part, never granted the much-touted Freedman's Bureau the authority to provide reparations for the years of free labor stolen from the slaves. When congressional resolve foundered on the economic rock of expropriating the plantations of Confederate whites and using the proceeds to provide blacks with "forty acres and a mule," blacks were left with neither the money nor the means necessary for survival in a still racially hostile world.

DOOR II. THE POST-CIVIL WAR AMENDMENTS

Radical Republicans committed to the Abolitionist cause pushed for the passage of the post-Civil War Amendments, which were designed to secure citizenship for the former slaves and to provide them with voting rights. Other statesmen realized that unless they acted to legitimate the freedman's status, Southerners would use violence to force blacks back into slavery, and the economic dispute that had precipitated the Civil War would surface again.

In an effort to avoid another conflict, and to secure Republican control of the Southern states, Congress enacted the Thirteenth, Fourteenth, and Fifteenth Amendments and the Civil Rights Acts of 1870-1875. Registering to vote in great numbers, blacks helped. But within a decade Southern planters rendered the Thirteenth Amendment obsolete by exercising raw economic power and using naked violence to establish a sharecropping system that provided them with the same labor benefits as slavery without the minimum obligations inherent in the slave master's role.

Although black men had gained the right to vote,

the federal government failed to enforce the Fifteenth Amendment for almost a century after its enactment. The Fourteenth Amendment, not passable as a specific protection for black rights, was finally enacted as a general guarantee of life, liberty, and property for all persons. Following a period of judicial ambivalence, corporations were deemed persons under the Fourteenth Amendment and for several generations received far more judicial protection than blacks. Indeed, blacks became the victims of judicial interpretations of the Fourteenth Amendment and of legislation construed so narrowly as to render the promised protection virtually meaningless.

Door III. Desegregation

Black people believed that *Brown v. Board of Education* was the greatest Supreme Court decision of all time. Certainly, it was a freedom symbol without equal in the long struggle for racial equality. Even though its promise of equality emanated more from its language than from its holding,[12] as they had with earlier symbols, blacks read the opinion for all it was worth and hoped for the best.

But the promise has proven elusive. The *Brown* decision, like its predecessors, is fading into the gloom, its message unfulfilled, its language of little use when pitted against the economic barriers that seriously dilute its potential. Good schools and decent housing remain beyond the financial reach of most of those who were the intended beneficiaries. In short, *Brown* and its judicial and legislative progeny have opened the door toward middle-class success for many, but have not touched those blacks still needing the modern-day equivalent of "forty acres and a mule."

DOOR IV. THE CIVIL RIGHTS ACTS OF 1964

The Civil Rights protest movement of the early 1960s developed out of the realization that court-mandated changes in the interpretation of the Constitution would not alone bring an end to racial segregation. Responding to the moral pressure exerted by courageous civil rights activists whose peaceful protests both embarrassed the nation and disrupted business in hundreds of cities and towns, Congress enacted legislation in 1964 to provide enforceable remedies for victims of racial discrimination in voting, employment, and access to public accommodations. While the obnoxious "Colored" and "White" segregation signs slowly disappeared, racial discrimination in voting, employment, even in access to public accommodations continued in forms both simplistic and sophisticated.

DOOR V. THE VOTING RIGHTS ACT OF 1965.

Southern states' determination to prevent blacks from exercising the basic citizenship right of suffrage remained firm despite the reform pressures of new federal laws. A massive effort by the Rev. Martin Luther King Jr.'s followers in Alabama and the vicious response of police officials, much of it documented on television, sparked Congressional action. The Voting Rights Act of 1965, signed by President Lyndon Johnson and quickly approved by the Supreme Court, provided civil rights lawyers with effective enforcement tools that, despite continuing resistance, resulted in thousands of new black voters whose ballots quickly increased the numbers of black, elected officials.

Resistance, though, did not end. Southern states shifted their defense from barring black voters to a host of techniques designed to dilute the black vote. The remedy that evolved over several years and dozens of voting rights cases, required establishment of majority black voting districts. Under this process, many more Blacks were elected to Congress and to state legislatures, but a conservative Supreme Court has again jeopardized black political gains by finding these districts in violation of the Constitution.

DOOR VI. AFFIRMATIVE ACTION

Frustration with the slow pace of desegregation in inner cities across the nation led to a series of urban rebellions in the late 1960s and early 1970s. While the heavy damage and loss of life was mainly confined to predominantly black areas, corporate, government, and institutional leaders, fearing more widespread disruption, instituted a series of efforts to bring in more blacks to colleges and employment opportunities which had been either closed to blacks or where only token numbers had been admitted.

Under these affirmative action policies as they came to be known, some of these programs worked better than others, but as the job market tightened and anxiety about their future well-being increased, more and more whites opposed these programs, whatever their effectiveness. This opposition was encouraged by politicians at every level, quite willing to win elections by blaming the nation's malaise on affirmative action programs. The Supreme Court's early support of these measures evaporated as public opposition grew.

oooooooo

Even the most determined pessimist must acknowledge the change in the racial landscape over the last century. But each door opened has revealed another barrier, less foreboding but still impenetrable. In a generation that promised the beginning of the golden age of opportunity for all blacks, their share of not only the good things, but also the essentials of life, has been drastically reduced for all but the most fortunate among them. Thus, despite breakthroughs, we find ourselves in the midst of an increasingly grim national scene. Black people are sinking deeper into the misery of unemployment, crime, broken families, and out-of-wedlock births, all indicia of an exploited, colonized people. These multitudes are without jobs, decent homes, and adequate education. Ironically, these same black people are protected by more expansive civil rights laws than any of their ancestors.

Because poor blacks remain outcasts in this country, the progress made by better-off blacks is always in jeopardy. The gap between the economic statistics for blacks and whites is hardly greater than that which exists between upper-class blacks and their poverty-level brethren. Blacks who have and those who have not are increasingly separated by neighborhood, schooling, employment, recreation, and even place of worship. Both groups are caught in the grip of an economic segregation as structured, and as harmful, as the law-enforced segregation that plagued their lives a generation ago.

Dr. King, in his last book, recognizing that civil rights progress had been slowed by a white backlash, urban riots, and other problems of the late 1960s, sought to reassure blacks with the explanation that:

[T]he line of progress is never straight. For a period a movement may follow a straight line and then it encounters obstacles and the path bends. It is like curving around a mountain when you are approaching a city. Often it feels as though you were moving backward, and you lose sight of your goal; but in fact you are moving ahead, and soon you will see the city again, closer by.[13]

It is a beautiful thought, elegantly expressed. But Dr. King's reassurance is now more than three decades old, and its continued applicability to the current condition of black people cannot ease our fears. The goal of equal opportunity that once loomed on the horizon like a heavenly city, is now seldom visible.

In the version of *Bluebeard's Castle* that Charles Perrault published, Judith's relatives arrive in time and slay Bluebeard. No possibility of a similar happy ending seems to exist in my analogous use of the fairy tale to gain an understanding of American racial policy. For here, the nation, like Bluebeard, is a mixture of all the evil in its history with all the potential for good in its national ideals. Neither Bluebeard nor this country is able to suppress the belief that, somehow, redemption may be gained without surrendering or even acknowledging spoils obtained through the most pernicious evil.

Bartok's *Bluebeard* manifests this hope for redemption without contrition in the opera's final scene. When Judith opens the seventh door and learns that Bluebeard has not murdered his former wives, they advance, proudly and slowly, in single file, splendidly adorned with their crowns and jewels.

They stop in front of Bluebeard. Then he, and not they, sinks to his knees. As in a dream and with open arms, he sings:

> *Lovely visions! Beauty tend you:*
> *Live in beauty, never ending!*
> *You have gathered all my riches;*
> *Wrought the fragrance of my garden;*
> *Brought me land and armed my power;*
> *Yours is my domain and being!*

Bluebeard's seeming homage to his wives is actually a reassertion of his power.

Similarly, the Emancipation Proclamation and the other documents of black freedom simulate a nation's concern about racial discrimination. Actually, the civil rights laws and policies are the fortuitous fall out of initiatives and policies that are important in the maintenance of white dominance.

And just as there is little reason to believe Judith will be Bluebeard's last attempt to regain his humanity through symbolic marriage and the inhumane sacrifice of another bride, I can find little basis for hope, either from history or by analogy from the fairy tale, that the racial pattern of freedom symbols for blacks and preservation of substantive power for whites.

America, too, has a Seventh Door. Behind it there is the potential for self-revelation for whites as well as blacks. Salvation for all is possible if its light can reveal the destructiveness of whiteness, can provide an antidote to its corrupting influence, a corrective for its mesmerizing hypnotic spell. The door will not be opened until blacks become insistent or when political or economic conditions dictate this long-overdue revelation.

And, if the door of racial revelation is thrown

open, there is certainly reason to expect that blacks and whites will be wary of what they learn from the light, will hesitate to risk reaching out and embracing the truth about a racial history that changes form but never alters its racial advantage for whites. Perhaps behind this door too, we will find a betrayal of our dreams for an end to this racial bondage. Disappointed, resigned to our fate, we will watch as it too, like Bluebeard's Judith, is retired to some somber chamber while the stage grows dark and the curtain falls.

Epilogue

"**I**t's time, friend. Our work here is ended."

I heard Geneva but did not answer. My mind was still on Judith. She married Bluebeard despite his reputation for evil and entered that gloomy castle with nothing to protect her, save faith that she could make a life there for them both. Her sad story certainly reflects the harshness of life for those early French peasants, lives with which a large percentage of people living in today's supposedly more humane world can identify.

"What's wrong?"

I sighed. "The themes in this final story are so stark and depressing. Judith's faith is no match for Bluebeard's obsession with power. Even her courage in trying to open the castle to sunlight is misconstrued. Bela Bartok's opera characterizes her as a too-inquisitive wife, subject to criticism rather than commendation because, surrounded with evil, she could not live her life under the pretense that evil did not exist."

"Judith's fate is far from unique," Geneva reminded.

"That too is a concern. Consider the other stories we're using to illustrate the *Afrolantica Legacies*. Tamar gave up her life in the Citadel in an effort to challenge its elitist, leadership selection policies. She failed and for her pains, she was banished. Paul Robeson dared both to speak out against racism and to link it to capitalist exploitation. Only his enemies really listened and their retaliation cost him his career, his reputation, and his health. Thurgood Marshall's life on the Supreme Court, for him a well-deserved pentacle of a brilliant legal career, was filled with frustration as his dozens of dissents duly note."

"But don't you see? Each challenge to wrongfully exercised power was an important event to the individuals making them and to those in the society who were motivated to mount challenges of their own."

"What I see, Geneva, is that we are holding out as models individuals who risked much in efforts to call attention to serious wrongs. And they all failed. Not exactly messages likely to challenge whatever How-to-Improve-Your-Life-in-Ten-Easy-Lessons book now topping the best seller lists."

"Pro—fes—sor." I could hear the exasperation in Geneva's voice. "The *Afrolantica Legacies* we've embellished with stories offer readers life-long rules of racial preservation, not short-term, feel-good fixes."

"I know that, but I am thinking of the millions for whom these messages will be drowned out by the seductive calls from an economic system that has them enthralled with the need to make it, the need to win at whatever the cost."

"Precisely why it is the right message, friend. Tamar, Paul Robeson, and Thurgood Marshall all acted as they did because, committed to justice and unable to abide evil, they responded to feelings that demanded action. In other words, they understood the essence of Jesus' advice to Peter."

"And that was?"

"It's not in any of the Gospels, at least not in so many words. Multitudes of people had gathered on a hillside to hear Jesus speak. One of the disciples, Peter, looked out at them, shook his head in despair and said, 'Master, they are so needy.'

'They do not truly understand what you are preaching. Many still worship idols and adhere to their old ways. They don't see the truth in the parables, Master, I fear it is hopeless—'

At this point, Jesus put his hand on Peter's shoulder

and said: 'Peter. Save thyself. The rest are mine.'"

I nodded. "A powerful story, Geneva. One that blurs the enormity of wrong in the world, while sharpening our focus on what each of us can do. Still, it's an easy message to lose sight of in the hurly-burly of a competitive world."

"Competition is not necessarily bad."

"No, but competition can become compulsive, an addiction really, one that encourages the taking of unfair advantage, exploiting, and worse."

"You're describing the human condition more than the temptations under a particular economic system."

"Perhaps. It's just that there seems no end to those who view power as license to abuse, sanction to exploit, invitation to demean. Will a time ever come when those with power believe in and practice justice? Is it so unreasonable to expect that one's work will be rewarded equitably, that there will be help in time of need, and recognition and regard for all—whatever their rank or status?"

"I think, friend, that both history and our experiences support a pessimistic response. But consider what you are asking for. Would you truly be happier in a perfect world, without challenge, without threat, without serious social problems?"

I thought for a long moment. "I would not choose a world of woe and the need to fight against unremitting evils as the necessary ingredients for a fulfilling life. Sure, I've been fortunate. My life has gained meaning from efforts to win rights for others. And in the process, I have been able to protect my sense of self in a society ever-ready to demean me and those who look like me. But, Geneva, it is tempting to imagine a time of widespread peace with justice, integrity and truth."

"It sounds like Camelot, and we know what happened even in fiction to King Arthur's idyllic land of brave knights and fair ladies."

Then, it struck me. "How about Afrolantica? How

does it differ from Camelot or Shangri-la, or any other imaginary paradise?"

"You've just said it. Afrolantica is not an imaginary paradise. It is real."

I looked at Geneva. She was quite serious.

"The Camelots, the Shangra-las, all are envisioned as escapes from the real world. Afrolantica is a reflection of that world, one offering a perspective that enlightens and encourages people wherever they are. That was the gift Afrolantica's black settlers gained as their promised land sank beneath the waves. How can you not see the difference? All the stories that we've done together over ten years, don't they mean anything to you?"

"Geneva!" Then I stopped, surprised by the tears in her eyes, the hurt in her voice. I remembered Nat T's warning: 'Man, don't you understand. In denying Geneva Crenshaw's, existence, you are denying your existence. There is no hope for you, man. No hope.'

I spoke quietly so as not to upset her any more than I had already. "The stories mean a lot to me. You mean a lot to me. But our stories, our friendship, even those powers of yours. They don't seem a match for the racial evils that are getting worse."

Her response was also quiet, almost a whisper. "Think of all the people who read the original "Afrolantica Awakening" story. The message they got from it about the importance of a homeland in their minds, in their hearts. It had nothing to do with whether there was or wasn't an Afrolantica."

I nodded my agreement.

"And our hope is that those who read the stories we have done here will gain understanding, and maybe some strength and inspiration to take on the tough problems."

"As the President is doing with Liberation Day?"

Geneva had already started gathering her belongings. "Yes, the President's commitment to address the costs of using whiteness as property will help. And so, I hope, will my response that the property value of whiteness is dependent on our recognizing it as such. But with or without the urging of highly placed persons, the need exists to understand this fundamental aspect of racism, to discuss it, to work to lessen its grip."

"Of course, you're right Geneva, but we have been preaching this message for a long time. As we saw in the Black Sedition Papers scenario, even our progressive writings can be used to justify our continued subordination. Our options, moreover, are limited. Chiara urged militant action, but such protests are difficult to mount or sustain in the present era of decreased expectations. Other groups, including those who have themselves suffered serious oppression, are as likely to use us as pawns in their own survival schemes rather than join with us as allies come what may."

Geneva stopped her packing, walked over and put her hands on my shoulders.

"You sound weary. I think you need the vacation you refuse to take."

"I am tired, but there may be insight in my fatigue. Nat T may be right about the need for violent disruption as the necessary prerequisite for change."

"Friend. None of the *Afrolantica Legacies* call for violence. Jesus created a revolution that has lasted for two millennia, and he did it as a peacemaker. At best, violent revolutions replace one evil with another—often worse."

"Our record of civil rights reform is hardly better, Geneva. Emancipation didn't abolish slavery. It changed its form. The same can be said for the legal and political reforms that followed it. Chiara, even from a distant planet, saw that."

"But she came here to try to understand what they couldn't observe from afar."

"Life is a struggle. Perhaps, as you said, it shouldn't

be. Perhaps, as you hope, it won't always be. But it is now. That's the fact. We have to decide whether and how to be involved."

"And you're right. There are many whites for whom getting and spending is their priority. A property right in whiteness serves as both advantage to enable success and a comfort when they fail. Some blacks, perversely, are able to use race in a similar fashion."

"The challenge couldn't be harder, Geneva."

"And," she added, "the prospects dimmer."

I shrugged and looked over at Geneva. "There is the compensation of a wonderful comrade, a true friend." I gave Geneva a hug. "Let's get back to the struggle."

Notes

Racial Liberation Day

1. Robert Heilbroner, "The Roots of Social Neglect in the United States," in *Is Law Dead?* 288, 296 (E. Rostow, ed. 1971).

2. See, e.g., David R. Roediger, *The Wages of Whiteness: Race and the Making of the American Working Class* (Verso, New York, 1991); Howard Winant, *Racial Conditions: Politics, Theory, Comparisons* (University. of Minnesota Press, Minneapolis, 1994); Noel Ignatiev, *How the Irish Became White*, (Routledge, New York 1995); Jane Lazarre, *Beyond the Whiteness of Whiteness: Memoir of a White Mother of Black Sons* (Duke University Press, 1996); Toni Morrison, *Playing in the Dark: Whiteness and the Literary Imagination* (Harvard University Press, 1992); Ian F. Haney Lopez, *White by Law: The Legal Construction of Race* (New York University Press, 1995); Eric J. Sundquist, *To Wake the Nations: Race in the Making of American Literature* (Belknap/Harvard, Cambridge, 1993).

3. Cheryl Harris, "Whiteness As Property," 106 *Harvard Law Review* 1707, 1713 (1993).

4. Ibid. at 1759.

5. Robert Reich, *Locked in the Cabinet* (Alfred Knopf, New York, 1997).

6. Edmund Morgan, *American Slavery, American Freedom* (W.W. Norton, New York, 1975)

7. See, e.g. Ken Emerson, *Doo Dah! Stephen Foster and the Rise of American Popular Culture* (Simon & Shuster, New York, 1997).

8. David Roediger, *When White Boys Want to Rap; Towards the Abolition of Whiteness* (Verso,

New York, 1994).

9. Jeremy Rifkin, *The End of Work* (G.P. Putnam, New York, 1995).

10. William Julius Wilson, *When Work Disappears: The World of the New Urban Poor* (Alfred Knopf, New York, 1996).

11. Carl T. Rowan, *The Coming Race War in America: A Wake-Up Call* (Little, Brown & Co., Boston, 1996).

12. Howard Winant, "Racial Dualism at Century's End," in *The House That Race Built: Black Americans, U.S. Terrain* (Wahneema Lubiano, ed., Pantheon Books, New York, 1997).

13. Stephen Thernstrom and Abigail Thernstrom, *America in Black and White*, 523-23 (Simon & Shuster, New York, 1997). *Beverly Daniel Tatum, Why Do All the Black Children Sit Together in the Cafeteria* (Basic Books, New York, 1997).

14. See, e.g., *Race Traitor*, a journal published in Cambridge, Massachusetts, that "aims to serve as an intellectual center for whites and others seeking to abolish the white race." Reported on in *Harper's*, Vol. 290, p. 17 (Mar. 1995).

15. Stephen Thernstrom and Abigail Thernstrom, *America in Black and White*, 523-26 (Simon & Shuster, New York, 1997).

16. Roberto Rodriguez and Patrisia Gonzales, "Time to Ponder 'White Question'," *The Houston Chronicle, Outlook* p. 1 (Apr. 20, 1997).

17. Pamela Burdman, "Scholars Gather in Berkeley to Talk About Whiteness: 3-day meeting on UC campus," *The San Francisco Chronicle* p. A7 (Apr. 12, 1997). Professor Michael Omi, one of the conference's faculty sponsors, said in response to criticism of the event: "'There's a growing interest in expanding the study of race to address whiteness,

which was at previous times transparent. We hope as a political consequence to bring to the forefront what white identity and politics are to make comprehensive links for groups that are trying to challenge racism."

18. Alice Walker, *Anything We Love Can Be Saved: A Writer's Activism* (Random House, New York 1997).

Chiara's Enlightenment

1. Frank Rich, "State Of Denial", *New York Times.* Page 21, col. 6, (Feb. 8, 1997).

2. See, e.g., Mari Matsuda and Charles Lawrence, *We Won't Go Back: Making the Case for Affirmative Action* (Houghton Mifflin, Boston, 1997).

3. Arthur Miller, "Pretense and Our Two Constitutions," 54 *Geo. Wash. L. Rev.* 375 (1986).

4. Brown vs. Board of Education, 347 U.S. 483 (1954).

5. Arthur Miller, "Social Justice and the Warren Court: A Preliminary Examination," 11 Pepperdine L. Rev. 473, 474 (1984).

6. Susan Strum and Lani Guinier, "The Future of Affirmative Action: Reclaiming the Innovative Ideal," 84 *California Law Review* 953 (1996).

7. Brown v. Board of Education, 347 U.S. 483 (1954).

8. Regents of the University of California v. Bakke, 438 U.S. 265 (1978).

9. See, e.g., Wygant v. Jackson Bd. of Educ., 106 S. Ct. 1842 (1986).

10. See e.g., Milliken v. Bradley, 418 U.S. 717 (1974).

11. See, e.g., United Steelworkers of America v. Weber, 443 U.S. 193 (1979) (white workers opposed

an apprenticeship program that the company would not have established in the absence of civil rights pressure because one-half of openings went to Blacks with lower seniority than some of whites).

Shadowboxing

1. Michael Cottman, "The Campus Radicals: Leonard Jeffries and other Afrocentric Professors refuse to whitewash their lesson plans," 5 *Emerge*, p. 26 (Feb. 1994).

2. The book, *The Secret Relationship Between Blacks and Jews*, was prepared by the Historical Research Department, Nation of Islam. It contains a quite controversial history of Jewish involvement in the Transatlantic slave trade and African slavery. This book was subjected to severe criticism by Professor Henry Louis Gates in a full-page, op-ed article titled, "Black Demagogues and Pseudo Scholars" published in the *New York Times* on July 20, 1993. A series of responses to this article, several of them quoted in this lecture, was published in 16 *Black Books Bulletin: WordsWork* (Winter 1993-1994). This Bulletin is published by Third World Press, Chicago, IL.

3. Cottman, supra note 1 at 28. The book is *The Jewish Onslaught: Dispatches from the Wellesley Battlefront.*

4. Paul Berman, "The Other and the Almost the Same," *The New Yorker* 61, 63 (Feb. 28, 1994).

5. Ibid.

6. Letty Cottin Pogrebin, "What Divides Blacks and Jews," New York *Newsday*, 48 (Mar. 2, 1994).

7. Ibid.

8. Minister Louis Farrakhan, *A Torchlight for America* (FCN Publishing, Chicago, 1993).

9. Ibid, at back cover.

10. Minister Louis Farrakhan, *Selected Speeches* (Joseph D. Eure and Richard M. Jerome eds, PC International Press, Philadelphia, 1989). See also, Florence Hamlish Levinsohn, *Looking for Farrakhan* (Ivan R. Dee, Chicago, 1997); Arthur J. Magida, *Prophet of Rage: A Life of Louis Farrakhan and His Nation* (Basic Books, New York, 1996).

11. Lynne Duke, "A Continuing 'Dialogue of Disagreement,'" *Washington Post* A6 (Feb. 28, 1994).

12. William Henry, III, "Pride and Prejudice," 143 *Time* 21, 23 (Feb. 28, 1994).

13. Haki Madhubuti, "Blacks, Jews and Henry Louis Gates, Jr" 16 *Black Books Bulletin* 3 (Winter 1993/1994).

14. Ibid., at 8.

15. Ibid.

16. Adolph Reed, *The Jesse Jackson Phenomenon: The Crisis of Purpose in Afro-American Politics*, 91 (Yale University Press, New Haven, 1986).

17. David Paterson, "White Outrage, Black Suspicion," *New York Times*, E. 17 (Mar. 20, 1994).

18. Ibid.

19. Pogrebin, supra, note 6.

20. Letty Cottin Pogrebin, "Ain't We Both Women? Blacks, Jews, and Gender," in *Deborah, Golda, and Me*, 275 (Crown Publishers, New York, 1991).

21. Michael Lerner, "The Real Crisis Is Selfishness," in 143 *Time*, 31, 34 (Feb. 28, 1994).

22. Micah Sifry, "Anti-Semitism in America," *The Nation* 92, 93 (Jan. 25, 1993).

23. Ibid., at 96.

24. Ibid.

25. Ibid., at 99.

Paul Robeson

1. See, e.g., Paul Robeson in Grolier Multimedia Encyclopedia for Windows (1997).
2. Derrick Bell, *Race, Racism, and American Law* (Little, Brown & Co., Boston, 1973).
3 Paul Robeson, *Here I Stand*, 36, 49 (Beacon Press, Boston, 1971).
4. Dorothy Gilliam, Paul Robeson: *All-American*, 158 (New Republic Books, Washington, 1976).
5. Martin Duberman, *Paul Robeson* 360-61, Knopf (New York, 1988).
6. Ibid., 394.
7. Paul Robeson, *Here I Stand*, 45-46 (Beacon Press, Boston, 1971).
8. Brown v. Board of Education, Brief for Appellants at 194.
9. Brown v. Board of Education, Amicus Curiae Brief for United States, p. 6.
10. W.E.B. Du Bois, *The Autobiography of W.E.B. Du Bois*, 333 (International Publishers, New York, 1968).
11. A. Blaustein and C. Ferguson, *Desegregation and the Law* 11-12 (1962).
12. Mary Duziak, "Desegregation as a Cold War Imperative," 41 Stan. L. Rev. 61, 63 (1988). Through an analysis of State Department and other government documents, Duziak found that the U.S. attorney General's office finally decided to throw its weight behind the NAACP Legal Defense Fund only when the State Department sent it various urgent messages requesting that it do so. 98-112.
13 Powell and Woods, "Jordan Most Popular

American" in Jet, p. 5, citing a Wall Street Journal/NBC news poll (May 19, 1997).

The Handmaid's Tale

1. Margaret Atwood, *The Handmaid's Tale*, (Houghton Mifflin, Boston, 1985).
2. Genesis 30: 1-3.
3. Audre Lorde, "The Master's Tools Will Never Dismantle the Master's House," *Sister Outsider*, (Trumansburg, New York, Crossing P, 1984).
4. *Black Judges on Judges*, Linn Washington, ed. (New Press, 1994).
5. Margaret Atwood, *The Handmaid's Tale*, 394-395 (Ballantine ed. 1985).
6. Ibid., at 390.
7. Speech of Justice Thurgood Marshall (Nov. 18, 1978), *The Barrister*, Jan. 15, 1979, at 1, reprinted in Derrick Bell, *Faces at the Bottom of the Well: The Permanence of Racism*, 63 (Basic Books, New York, 1987).
8. Ibid., at 252.
9. Ibid. at 273-73.
10. Carl T. Rowan, *Dream Makers, Dream Breakers: The World of Justice Thurgood Marshall*, 453 (1993).
11. Ibid. 453-54.
12. Ibid.
13. Ibid.

The Black Sedition Papers

1. Derrick Bell, *Confronting Authority: Reflections of an Ardent Protester*, 157 (Basic Books, New York, 1994).
2. Orlando Patterson, "Blacklash," in

Transition 62 (New Series V 3N4, 1993, W.E.B. Du Bois Institute for Afro-American Research, Harvard University, Cambridge, MA 02138).

3. Derrick Bell, "The Black Sedition Papers," in 66 *Transition* 107 (1995, W.E.B. Du Bois Institute for Afro-American Research, Harvard University, Cambridge, MA 02138).

4. Franz Fanon, *The Wretched of the Earth* (1961; Eng. trans., 1968), in which Fanon called for revolutions to liberate Third World peoples from dehumanizing colonialism.

5. [cite to responses to *NY Times* op-ed piece for f/n 6].

6. Orlando Patterson, "Race, Gender and Liberal Fallacies," *NY Times*, Oct. 20, 1991, Sec.4, p. 15, c. 2 (suggesting that if Clarence Thomas did, as Anita Hill asserted, make sexually suggestive overtures to her, he was justified in lying about it because he acted in the context of cultural norms well known, particularly to Southern black women from working-class backgrounds).

7. Cheryl Harris, "Whiteness as Property," 106 *Harvard Law Review* 1710 (1993).

Bluebeard's Castle: An American Fairytale

1. *Encyclopedia Britannica* 11th ed., s.v. "Bluebeard."

2. *Encyclopedia Britannica* 7th ed., s.v. "Perrault." The tale is attributed to Charles Perrault, a seventeenth-century French poet, prose writer, and storyteller. He was a prominent member of the Academie Francaise, and wrote fairy stories, actually updated versions of half-forgotten folk stories, to amuse his children. In addition to *Bluebeard's Castle*, his stories include *Little Red Riding Hood,*

The Sleeping Beauty, and *Puss in Boots.*
3. See Bela Bartok, *Bluebeard's Castle,*
Columbia Records recording 1963, MS 6425.
4. Robert Darnton, *The Great Cat Massacre
And Other Episodes in French Cultural History* (Basic
Books, New York, 1984)
5. Ibid at 33.
6. Ibid.
7. Emancipation Proclamation, No. 17, 12 Stat.
1268 (1863).
8. U. S. Const, Amend XIV. U.S. Const,
Amend XIII.
9. Civil Rights Act of 1964, Pub. L. No. 88-352,
78 Stat. 241 (codified as amended in scattered sec-
tion of 42 U S Const); Voting Rights Act of 1965,
Pub. L. No. 89-110, 79 Stat. 437 (codified as
amended in scattered sections of 42 U S Const);
Fair Housing Act of 1968, Pub. L. No. 90-284, 82
Stat. 81 (codified as amended in scattered sections
of 42 U S Const).
10. See, e.g., R. Allen, *Black Awakening in
Capitalist America* (1969), racism used to maintain
black America as a domestic colony of white
America. M. Berry, *Toward Freedom and Civil Rights
for the Freedom: Military Policy Origins of the
Thirteenth Amendment and the Civil Rights Act of
1866* (1975); maintaining that the Thirteenth
Amendment was prompted less by the desire to free
blacks generally than the necessity of placating and
then disarming large numbers of black troops
recruited during the period. Morgan, *American
Slavery, American Freedom* (1975); a study of slavery
in early colonial Virginia indicating that elements of
both prejudice and profit were present in the slavery
equation, with emphasis on the latter.
11. See A. Zilversmith, *The First Emancipation:*

The Abolition of Slavery in the North (1967). reviewing the economic factors that undergirded efforts to abolish slavery in the northern states in the years following the Revolutionary War. Lynd, "Slavery and the Founding Fathers," in *Black History* 119 (M. Drimmer ed. 1968); reflecting the founding fathers' debate over slavery and their inability to overcome the sense that a nation conceived to protect property should not destroy property interest in slaves. All the above authorities and more are collected and discussed in D. Bell, *Race, Racism, and American Law* passim (2nd ed. 1980).

12. Having raised the hopes of blacks to heavenly levels, the Court then deferred relief until further arguments could be held, a departure from the usual process of granting immediate relief for the violation of personal constitutional rights. The following year, the Court rejected NAACP petitions for immediate relief, and returned the cases to the district courts with instructions requiring that "defendants make a prompt and reasonable start toward full compliance with our May 17, 1954, ruling." *Brown vs. Board of Educ.*, 349 U.S. 294, 300 (1995).

13. M. L. King, supra note 24, at 12.

Acknowledgments

I am both pleased and honored that Haki Madhubuti, founder and publisher of Third World Press, selected this fourth book of Geneva Crenshaw stories as part of the celebration marking TWP's three decades of providing communities of color with art, information, and the truth about life in this alien land we call home.

I want to thank Janet Dewart Bell who encouraged this project and read, reviewed, and discussed with me every word. My thanks as well to Gwendolyn Mitchell, my official editor whose careful editing and suggestions strengthen the book's structure and its stories. Phoebe Hoss, who edited each of my earlier trade books kindly read the manuscript and offered helpful comments. Deborah Creane did the same. Stacey Schwartz, an NYU law student, and Paulette Robinson provided helpful insights on the chapter addressing Jewish/black differences. Beverly Daniel Tatum, Frances Kendall, Jacqueline Green, Aliah Mubarak-Tharpe and Maggie Potapchuk, each suggested approaches for moving whites beyond white privilege that I tried to incorporate in President Clinton's speech on race.

I want to acknowledge publications where earlier versions of some of these essays appeared or are forthcoming.

Afrolantica—"The Afrolantica Awakening" in *Faces at the Bottom of the Well*: The Permanence of Racism (Basic Books, New York, 1992).

Chiara's Enlightenment—"Xerces and the

Affirmative Action Mystique," (A tribute to Prof. Arthur S. Miller) 57 *Geo. Wash. L. Rev.* 701 (1989).

Shadowboxing: Blacks, Jews, and Games Scapegoats Play—forthcoming; The Farrakhan Factor: African American Writers on Leadership, Nationhood and Minister Louis Farrakhan, Amy Alexander, ed., (Grove Press, New York, 1997).

The Citadel—*Confronting Authority: Reflections of an Ardent Protester* (Beacon Press, Boston, 1994).

Paul Robeson: Doing the State Some Service—forthcoming; Paul Robeson: Icon and Hero, (Paul Robeson Cultural Center, Rutgers, The State University of New Jersey).

The Black Sedition Papers—"The Black Sedition Papers," in 66 *Transition* 107 (1995, W.E.B. Du Bois Institute for Afro-American Research, Harvard University, Cambridge).

Bluebeard's Castle: An American Fairy Tale—An American Fairy Tale: The Income-Related Neutralization of Race Law Precedent, 18 *Suffolk University. Law Review* 331 (Fall, 1984).